THE
HARBORMASTER

RENEE GARRISON
WITH ROBERT GARRISON

Praise for *The Harbormaster*

This is not another conventional mystery set against an exotic backdrop. Baxter—who visits strip clubs, meets with forensics experts, and traces phone calls during his bouts of amateur sleuthing—is a man deeply involved in the fragile ecosystem of the marina, allowing the setting to become as important as the crime itself. *The Harbormaster* was inspired by real events, and the Garrisons write with obvious affection for boating communities and marina life, filling the novel with lived-in details about storms, fuel docks, maintenance work, and the unpredictability of life spent near water. At times, these descriptive passages can start to meander, but the authors quickly bring the narrative back into focus.

Despite its grisly central crime, *The Harbormaster* ultimately evokes a genuine sense of warmth and community. Baxter's loving and playful relationship with his wife, Harri, gives the novel an emotional core, while the eccentric dockside characters provide humor and charm. There's something infectious about the calm energy with which Baxter moves through the novel's events. Even after the mystery is solved, what lingers is not the sensational details of the crime, but the desire to inhabit this unhurried world for a little while longer.

—BookLife

THE HARBORMASTER

RENEE GARRISON
WITH ROBERT GARRISON

nrk
designs

Florida

ISBN: 979-8-9916874-8-5 (paperback)
ISBN 979-8-9916874-9-2 (ebook)
Library of Congress Control Number: 2026909400

To request permission contact
Renee Garrison, reneegarrison2@gmail.com

Edited by:
Anne C. Jacob, Popin Edits, https://AnneCJacob.com

Cover design and page layout by:
Nancy R. Koucky, NRK Designs, https://nrkdesigns.com

Cover Photo by Robert Garrison

NRK Designs Publishing
Florida
Printed in United States of America

We dedicate this book to boats, boaters,
and the marinas where they congregate—
especially along the coasts of Florida. Aboard a boat, we can feel
closer to the adventurers and explorers who were captivated by
the beauty of the Sunshine State
long ago and continue to preserve
their vision of paradise.

PROLOGUE

Marina docks are magical at night.

Thin halyards strum against sailboat masts, accompanied by a chorus of crickets. Shadows with form, with substance, appear in the moonlight, stealing kisses and soft caresses. The enchantment of darkness brings a sense of privacy, a pleasurable distance from daily life.

Beneath the canopy of stars, a dolphin breaks the surface of the water—a silent witness to the humans stepping aboard the boat. Tonight, each comforting creak of wooden deck boards draws a couple further away from their responsibilities. As the vessel rocks, gentle waves radiate across the water. The animal watches, curious about the activity near its nocturnal feeding ground. But it need not be concerned.

By morning, one of the lovers will be dead.

CHAPTER 1

As I watched a brilliant sunrise, the boat exploded. Looking skyward, I hadn't noticed the boat drifting in our channel. I *heard* it instead.

Ka-boom!

I jumped as flames obliterated the sky. For a brief moment, my feet refused to move. Grabbing the cell phone from my pocket, I punched in 911. As I explained the situation to an operator, I looked toward the water where the boat was blazing and read the name scrawled across its transom. *Feelin' Nauti.*

Marina finished her kibble and stared out my office window, purring at the inferno. She looked back at me and blinked.

Rifling through my files, I located the owner's name and phone number. He was a doctor, so I knew he would be up, getting ready to make rounds at the hospital. He answered on the second ring and listened silently, shocked at the news. After a long pause, he mumbled an unexpected reply.

"Uh, I guess I should warn you, I kept guns and ammo aboard."

"What kind of guns?"

"An AK-47, a handgun, and about two thousand rounds of ammunition."

I closed my eyes, hoping that when I opened them, I'd be awake, and this nightmare would end. I've never owned a gun, but I was fairly certain heat could ignite bullets. I snapped myself back into reality, ended the call, and walked out to the dock to wait for the fire department.

The sun's first streak of light glistened across the water, which meant some of my marina residents would be rising, too. I didn't want any of them to be struck by a stray bullet. Tom McDonald, a retired sheriff, lived aboard his sailboat. I figured he'd know enough to duck.

"I wish I had some marshmallows and chocolates. We could make s'mores."

Gordon, the boatyard manager, stood beside me, coffee in hand. We heard the wail of sirens approaching.

"That's one hell of a wake-up call, Cap'n Mac."

"It might get even better," I said, explaining about the bullets.

Gordon's head jerked quickly, and his coffee sloshed in the cup. "Looks like a salvage job, to me, buddy. No need to get any closer to save the vessel."

"Absolutely no intention of it, my friend."

A fire truck screeched to a halt in the parking lot. Men lumbered down the dock in large rubber boots.

I stepped forward. "Good morning. I'm Baxter McCracken, the harbormaster here at Moss Creek Marina."

As I briefed the man in charge, his expression changed to disbelief. "Hell, I'm not taking my men out to a boat that's loaded with live ammunition." He folded beefy arms across his chest.

Flames inside the boat erupted—along with a few gunshots—the result of heat igniting the ammunition.

I walked back to my office, grabbed my clipboard, and headed to the fuel pump. Even a burning boat couldn't keep me from my daily tasks. Part of my job involves tracking how much fuel is sold and how much remains in the tank, so I know when to order more and make sure we're not losing any fuel due to leaks or theft.

Yet it was hard to concentrate with police officers barking on a public address system and a helicopter circling above, trying to determine whether anyone was on board the flaming boat.

One policeman joined me on the dock and nodded. "Funny thing, we got a call from the owner's wife not long ago to report that a woman was on that boat who had been harassing her and her family. Said her husband had been having an affair with this stripper, and she had been living on their boat for a few weeks."

I raised one eyebrow, which he probably couldn't see behind my sunglasses. "Really? I haven't seen any activity aboard, but I'll check with my dockmaster who worked the weekend shift."

In addition, I checked with the marina owner. Peter Johnson was a lawyer who amassed a fortune from personal injury cases. His own boat had been docked at the marina for years, and when he heard the place was for sale, he bought it. Peter was at his law firm on the day *Feelin' Nauti* was brought into the yard.

He answered my call with professional aloofness that quickly shifted to annoyance upon hearing about the fire. "Hell, I haven't seen anyone aboard that boat. We don't need this kind of publicity. If anyone from the media approaches you, do not comment. Direct them to me."

"Roger that." A few news vans were parked in the marina lot, so I spent the rest of the day avoiding men and women carrying microphones or notebooks. It wasn't hard to do since I normally wear a hat with a large brim for full shade coverage following melanoma surgery on my temple. I doubt that my own mother would recognize my face when I'm wearing my sun protective hat.

When I got home, Harri emerged from her office and watched me pour myself a "Florida Man" double IPA from Cigar City Brewing. She kissed me. "Tell me about your day."

My wife, Harriet McCracken, is a former newspaper reporter-turned-columnist who worked remotely via computer. She writes about a variety of topics, usually with insight and a dash of sarcasm. Her sense of humor drew me to her when she was a nineteen-year-old customer at the Orlando bank where I worked as a manager. That and a pair of long, shapely legs that still turn heads thirty years later.

"You wouldn't believe my day. By any chance, have you watched the local news on television?"

She frowned. "You know how I loathe those talking heads. Never trust the opinion of anyone who speaks in sound bites and pauses for commercial breaks."

I held up my palms in surrender. "I understand that print journalism provides citizens with the information they need to make the best possible decisions about their lives, their communities, their societies, and their governments. But this is one instance that you've just got to *watch*."

We settled on the couch, and I searched for the local news station. Moments later, the blazing boat burst onto the screen.

Harri rubbed my shoulders as she watched. When the segment ended, she turned her head. "That event is probably not a great addition to your resume, my dear harbormaster."

I yawned. "Neither is my forty-year career in banking nor my volunteer work for the Red Cross. Somehow, I cope."

A hot shower and a change of clothes left me refreshed and suddenly starving. To my delight, I found two filet mignons resting on the kitchen counter.

Harri grinned. "I had a craving for meat."

"And here I am."

"I am a lucky woman indeed. You can cook."

Her arms encircled my waist as I set a cast-iron skillet over high heat until it began to smoke. After coating the steaks with salt and a generous amount of coarsely ground black pepper, I placed them in the skillet and left them alone for two and a half minutes. When the cooked side turned a deep, golden brown, I flipped them over for two more minutes. Then the skillet slid into the oven for six minutes, which produced steaks done to medium-rare perfection. I added two tablespoons of Irish butter—a nod to my red-headed grandmother—plus a clove of garlic and a sprig of thyme to the pan, spooning it gently over the meat.

Slicing into a crispy baked potato, Harri asked, "Do you think the stripper really set fire to her lover's boat? Hell hath no fury . . ."

". . . like a woman scorned. And how would you know about scorned women?"

She smiled. "I have interviewed so many of them."

CHAPTER 2

MARINA, THE CAT, WAS WAITING at my office door with a dead lizard in her jaws when I arrived.

"A present for me? How delightful."

She darted past me toward her food dish as I dropped the lizard in the trash. I counted the cash in the marina office drawer to make sure it balanced. The coffee had just finished brewing when a policeman from the day before walked in and helped himself to a cup.

"We were supposed to evict a female squatter from the boat, *Feelin' Nauti*, this week at the owners' request, but that was before it began drifting in the channel." He added enough sugar to the cup to make Willy Wonka retch.

"Lucky for us, it didn't float far, possibly because it was dragging an anchor. By the time the fire was extinguished, and our officers boarded the boat, they found the woman had gone."

"Obviously, she was not an experienced boater."

The policeman chuckled. "*Obviously*, Cap'n Mac.

I just stopped by to take another look at the scene."

"No problem. We've got a salvage contractor working on it now, pulling off deck hardware, winches, blocks, and cleats. None of the stainless steel was damaged by the fire, and the exterior of the boat survived in fine condition. They've already removed the mast, boom, and standing rigging."

"The initial report says it appears that someone set a small fire on deck." He refilled his coffee and shook his head in disbelief.

"Maybe flaming batons are part of her stage act?"

"I should check it out. Professionally, of course." He grinned.

After the policeman left, I began the tedious task of counting inventory. Every cola can, sunscreen, soap, razor, Baby Ruth, and Butterfinger bar had to be accounted for. The owner of the marina was paranoid about potential theft. I'd just finished when the legal eagle himself walked in.

"The marina has been all over the news," Peter said, running a hand through his hair. "My doctor friend, Alberto Raffo, is furious. You know it was his boat that was torched."

"I do. I placed the call that morning to alert him. Such a terrible thing."

He looked up. "The burned boat or the stripper that was rumored to be on board it?"

I struggled to maintain a somber expression. "Both."

He stood at the window, staring at the fuel dock. "Remember, if you get any calls, direct the reporters to me."

"It will be my pleasure, Peter."

He disappeared down the dock, heading for *High Anxiety,* his vintage cruising yacht, which had been designed by a famous naval architect. It was a beautiful boat, but like anything old, the vessel required lots of repairs. New starters, fuel injectors, water pumps . . . The joke in our boatyard was that every time Peter turned the key in the ignition, it cost him $10,000. On rare occasions when the boat was running, he took his wife and their two college-age children on holiday cruises to the Bahamas.

Peter's kids worked shifts for me during their breaks from college. His daughter, Angela, was a slim, athletic-looking girl with long brown hair and a sweet smile. She learned procedures quickly and was efficient as a dockmaster, unlike her younger brother, who was polite with customers but a failure at any sort of record-keeping. I've never been sure if his lackadaisical attitude stemmed from an actual learning disability or simply that he would rather be surfing than working. In either case, I couldn't fire him.

"Nepotism at its finest," Harri murmured after meeting them at the marina holiday party. "Daddy will provide."

I picked up the handheld VHF radio along with my

keys and headed out to make rounds, an important part of managing a marina. With over seventy boats at the docks at any given time, there would always be at least one that needed its lines, fenders, or power cord adjusted. In addition, I checked for fuel leaks. Winds, tides, and currents love to play games with boats.

I noticed a fifty-foot Sportfisherman listing slightly to starboard. After checking her lines and finding nothing amiss, I climbed aboard. Her owner hid the keys to the cabin in a locker on deck. I let myself in and checked the bilge for any standing water. There were none, but two brand new starting batteries were waiting to replace the old ones. The additional weight was just enough to cause the boat to list, but no reason for concern, so I moved on to complete the rest of my inspection.

My rounds ended at the boatyard, and I dropped the daily operating report off at Gordon's office. Along with the policeman, Gordon was watching the salvage crew remove the last bits of hardware from the burned sailboat. Remarkably, the hull still looked perfect—like a giant nautical firepit.

One of the crew ventured into the charred cabin, and moments later, I heard a strangled scream and a shout. "Holy shit! Somebody get down here."

The policeman ran, with Gordon and me flanking him like a jet formation. We scrambled aboard, the smell of soot and smoke still overwhelming. Below deck, a man stood gripping one end of a long bench cushion. At the opposite end, long strands of black hair dangled in the still air, still attached to the remains of a charred scalp.

CHAPTER 3

BACK AT MY OFFICE, I tried to wash away the lingering smoky odor with salt air and strong coffee. The policeman immediately banished everyone from the boat, which was now considered a potential crime scene. Spotting the lint roller I keep on my desk, I attacked the seat cushions of each chair in the room. Marina naps in every one of them throughout the day and leaves a generous amount of her cat hair behind. To keep allergies at bay—both mine and my customers'—I removed it as often as possible.

I decided to ask Noah if he noticed anything unusual during his 11 p.m. to 7 a.m. shift. Noah and his wife lived at the marina aboard a thirty-four-foot boat, which they'd recently purchased. He'd been a pro surfer, but drug-related arrests derailed his career. When he asked about working as a dockmaster part-time, Peter agreed to hire him. "Everyone has a past and deserves a second chance," he'd said.

Noah's wife came from a banking background but

was currently employed in logistics for a large corporation, which provided a steady income. I liked them both, and having a live-aboard couple in the marina overnight added two sets of eyes for security.

As I made my rounds, I stopped at their boat and hoped Noah was still awake. He was sipping a beer on the aft deck.

"Just checking to see if you spotted anything—or anyone—out of the ordinary last night."

"No, sir." He lit a cigarette and exhaled. "It was a quiet night, but I wasn't the one on duty. Peter's daughter, Angela, worked the overnight shift. But hey, as long as we're talking, I forgot to tell you that a marina guest complained about bedbugs in the boater's lounge to me earlier."

Really? The boater's lounge shared a wall with my office. Theoretically, the bugs would migrate, but I didn't have any bites. The lounge contained a couch, chairs, and a laundry room for guests of the marina to use after a day on the water. Shelves stocked with books and boating magazines provided a diversion on rainy days. In truth, the place never got much use, so where could bedbugs come from?

I walked back to investigate and glanced at the television mounted on the wall. "A missing, suicidal woman last believed to be aboard a blazing boat has been discovered dead inside the vessel today," the news reporter intoned.

"State fire marshal investigators found the body on an interior bench beneath a cushion, according to a police spokesman. Fire damage concealed her remains from first responders during their search of the 1979 Morgan sailboat."

He added that, according to the local police chief, the woman's death "appeared to be a suicide."

Back in my office, I Googled "exterminators" and hired the only guy who would be available tomorrow. My coffee was cold, so I rinsed and replaced my clean mug on a shelf above the sink. It was part of a collection of odd drinking vessels that included a merry snowman, Valentine hearts, and a *Boston is for Lovers* cup. They were part of the odds and ends that accumulate in an office, abandoned and forgotten when their owners moved on to other jobs.

As I turned the office key in its lock and headed for my rounds, I heard my name.

"Cap'n Mac."

Behind me, a diver wearing scuba gear bobbed in the water beside the seawall.

"Could you do me a favor and distract this guy?" He nodded at the large manatee beside him.

"I've been hired to clean this boat hull, and he keeps bumping into me, trying to eat the plants I'm scraping off. He must think I'm his personal chef."

I smiled. "I've got the perfect distraction. No problem."

Seagrass beds growing along the seawall provided habitats for manatees, sea turtles, and juvenile fish. They also stabilized sediments and improved water clarity, so we were lucky to have them at Moss Creek Marina. A few yards away, I turned on a rubber hose, and the manatee followed, rolling over on his back to drink the fresh water. I got a quick thumbs-up from the diver before he disappeared below the surface.

Watching those "chubby mermaids," as they are nicknamed, was one of my favorite aspects of life in the Sunshine State. I'm a native Floridian—one of those few people whose family goes back five generations. I was born in Tampa long before Walt Disney bought citrus groves and cattle land outside of Orlando. I've watched natural, quiet environments replaced by a network of highways, shopping centers, and suburban communities. That's one of the reasons I love working at a historic marina.

Yet one of my *least* favorite aspects of this job was evicting boat owners for failing to pay their dockage fees. Many of them owned a lot of other toys—expensive motorcycles and exotic sports cars—but were chronically late with dockage, if they paid at all. This afternoon, I arranged for a thirty-five-foot Sea Ray to be towed out of the marina for non-payment, despite the owner crying in my ear over the phone, "But I have no gas in the tanks to move the boat. I've been a good customer. I can't believe this is happening to me."

Me neither, buddy.

Near the end of my shift, Harri called. "It's terribly hot, and I don't feel like cooking, but I have a brilliant idea. Why don't I meet you at The Place Next Door for dinner?"

The Place Next Door was a waterfront restaurant adjacent to my marina that featured exceptional seafood, service, and prices. "That sounds perfect. You're a genius."

"I know. That's the reason why you married me."

"As I recall, your legs also had something to do with it."

Later, I spotted Harri at the bar and greeted her with a kiss. She ordered a double martini, "Titos straight up with extra olives—stuffed with garlic if you have them. And please, just whisper the word *vermouth* in the glass."

She squeezed my hand. "I had a little free time this morning, so I did some online research. Court records show that Alberto and his wife each filed injunctions for protection against one Nikki Smith, a young woman who listed her occupation as an exotic dancer, earlier this year. Her presence in the Raffos' life does not seem to be a recent phenomenon."

I picked up my menu, but I couldn't focus on the food. Facts started to tangle themselves in my brain like an old fishing net snagged on a propeller.

CHAPTER 4

One of the many daily tasks at the marina involves sticking the tanks. Translated, that means checking the level of fuel in the underground storage tanks. The marina has a 10,000-gallon tank for diesel fuel as well as a 5,000-gallon tank for marine-formulated gasoline. I must be sure that no tank is leaking and no fuel has been stolen. It's an old-school process—no high-tech monitoring gadgets, just an old-fashioned fourteen-foot wooden stick.

I opened the fill caps (lever clamps on two sides and padlocked shut) and dropped the stick, measuring the fuel in inches. Fifty inches of fuel equals 5,000 gallons, so I checked fuel sales from yesterday, as well as fuel deliveries, to be sure the numbers added up properly. A discrepancy means trouble, and the owner won't be happy.

State of Florida inspectors are very particular about how our records are maintained. Underground fuel tanks adjacent to navigable waterways are a high priority. Fortunately, we have no problems. Relieved, I headed to the boater's lounge to clean up before the exterminator arrived. The term *lounge* made the place sound glamorous, but it wasn't. Every piece of furniture in the room was left behind by some yacht owner who donated it after they redecorated their main salon. An array of old boating magazines was piled on a wicker cocktail table, beside discarded paperback books that fill time on rainy days. The only real amenity offered was an adjacent laundry room, where the fragrance of detergent and fabric softener occasionally seeped into my dockmaster's office, too.

After tossing some used paper cups, I pulled the back cushions off the couch and shook them, looking for critters. That's when I spotted it—a Ziplock bag filled with powder. White powder. Running my hand between the seat cushions, I found three more. This didn't look good, so I called Tom McDonald, a retired sheriff currently living aboard a 42-foot, old Grand Banks yacht, and asked him to meet me in the lounge.

Minutes later, he strolled in. "Morning, Cap'n Mac. Got any fresh coffee?"

He stared at the bags in my hands. "I'm guessing that's not creamer and sugar."

"Me too, since it was stashed between the couch cushions. Does make me wonder if we're selling something besides boat fuel here."

His eyebrow raised. "Better tell the ambulance chaser."

The "ambulance chaser," as Tom calls Peter, refers to attorneys who chase actual ambulances, trying to speak to accident victims. Peter had minions who did it for him, along with an absurd amount of television ads to attract clients. Today, he happened to be working on his own boat and taking a break from the law. I climbed aboard and showed him the bags with a brief description of their location in the lounge.

His eyes widened. "Jesus, first the boat explosion and now drugs?"

"Do you think the two are related?"

Peter splayed his hand over his eyes and squeezed his temples. Either he suddenly experienced shooting pains in his skull, or he simply found the possibility of illegal drug trafficking in his marina excruciating. "I don't know, but I *do* know we are *not* reporting this to the police."

Sensing my surprise, he extended a used-car-salesman arm all the way around my shoulders. "Mac, it's like this. We don't need any more bad publicity, and I think we can solve this ourselves. Remember, very few people have access to the lounge, and they need a code for the door lock."

He owned the place, so I agreed. But I was not convinced that it would be the best course of action. The bedbug story flashed in my mind and I wondered if it was intended as cover for illicit activity. Did Noah deliberately spread the rumor to keep people away from the lounge?

I considered calling Harri to debate the point, but it was mid-afternoon and I realized she was probably at Starbucks. It's where she goes when she's anxious or has a bad case of writer's block. She said a chocolate croissant organizes her thoughts, and I'm grateful for that. There are worse ways to self-medicate.

I was reviewing dockage agreements when Angela arrived for her shift. The boss's daughter reminded me of my own, and I was happy to have her working for me at the marina during her college breaks. Like her brother, she loved to surf, and her deep tan reflected the hours spent in the water. She traveled to Mexico, Vietnam, and Australia in search of the perfect wave. The Beach Boys could have written a song about her. Had she been born decades earlier, she might have been called a flower child. *Unlike* her brother, Daniel, who spent much of his time dreaming of becoming a yacht photographer and flying his drone camera over the vessels docked at my marina, the girl was intelligent and personable. Angela was nothing like her parents, and I once wondered if they had adopted her.

"Hi, Angela. How are you today?"

She wore denim shorts and a slightly faded marina tee shirt. I smiled because I knew that her mother would be appalled by her appearance. Peter's wife, Claire, was a chic, moneyed woman, toned from years of dieting and exercise. She wore her hair in a shining black bob, with any trace of gray painstakingly concealed. Her lips were painted a perfect shade of red, and she frequently wore silk scarves with expensive labels tied around her neck, which Harri once explained is excellent for concealing the ravages of time to the delicate skin there.

"I'm good, thanks." She smiled. "Actually, I'm a little weirded out by that boat fire. Did they find out who did it?"

Her large brown eyes looked worried.

"I haven't heard anything yet, but your dad might know. Did he tell you the police found a body aboard?"

"A—*what*? No, he didn't say anything. Oh, my God."

She looked frightened, so I assured her that we were safe working at the marina and that the fire appeared to be the result of a standard love triangle—a jealous wife, a young mistress, and a philandering husband.

"Revenge can be weird," she said quietly. "I had a chemistry teacher once who brought pictures of her ex-boyfriend for us to burn over a Bunsen burner after they broke up."

Envisioning such a scene had me momentarily distracted before I remembered the question I needed to ask her.

"Angela, when you were on duty that night, did you notice anyone in the boater's lounge, did you see people going in or coming out?"

She chewed the inside of her lip and concentrated.

"No, I didn't, but honestly, someone could have gone in while I was making rounds. My brother was here for a while, playing with his drone, before he worked the 11 p.m. to 7 a.m. shift. Why do you ask? Does it have something to do with the boat explosion?"

I chose my words carefully. "I don't think so. We just found some stuff in the lounge, and we wondered who it belongs to."

She nodded, satisfied with my explanation. "Maybe we should start a lost and found box here at the marina."

I smiled and nodded back. Plastic bags filled with drugs don't really qualify for that.

CHAPTER 5

SEEING THE SUN RISE EVERY morning still steals my breath away. Today, it was a golden hue that reminded me of a caution signal. A welcome gust of cool air whisked the warmth from my skin as I walked from the parking lot to the dockmaster's office. I sucked in a breath through my teeth that made my gums tingle.

The overnight shift brewed a fresh pot of coffee before he left. I filled a *Merry Christmas* mug and heard the coffee hiss as a few drops hit the heating plate. The last week didn't seem real—any of it. A burning boat, a dead body, and bags of illegal drugs in the boater's lounge . . . What could happen next? Pirates of the Caribbean?

Gordon, the boatyard manager, arrived holding a paper bag that smelled so good Marina raised her head from the chair and sniffed.

"My friend, have you come bearing gifts?"

Gordon chuckled and handed me a warm guava pastry, fresh from the Cuban cafe down the street. "You provide the coffee and I provide the breakfast, Captain."

Marina leaped on the counter and watched me intently. I offered her a flaky fragment.

"Thank you, but I'd be grateful if you could also provide me with some answers about the boat and the body. Have you heard any talk in the boatyard?"

He blew on the steaming coffee in his China Valentine cup and shook his head. "They're talking alright, but they're clueless about what happened. Just a lot of guessing, I'm afraid. The doc who owns the boat has been a bit of a jerk around the yard when he's needed any work done. His wife isn't much better, although she just never speaks to any of us. Can't say there's a lot of sympathy for either of them. In fact, just the opposite."

"I know we don't employ a lot of altar boys to scrape hulls and weld metal, but have you seen any drugs around there? I found a few surprise packages in the boater's lounge."

Gordon wiped a bit of jelly from his beard. "I had one guy refuse to go to the emergency room after he got hurt. Evidently, he knew that he couldn't pass the drug test they administer in workmen's compensation claims. But the guys in the yard clear out at five o'clock, and they have no reason to be in the boaters' lounge. I mean, you would notice if they were in there, right? That place is for paying yacht customers. If I were dealing, I'd do it at night when fewer people are around."

I nodded and poured the crumbs from the pastry bag into Marina's food dish. "An excellent point. The culprit must be here at night. Do you suppose the stowaway stripper might have started adding to her IRA with illegal income?"

Gordon grinned. "Captain, I'm no expert, mind you, but I've heard that dancers and drugs go together like cops and donuts. But enough chitchat, as much as I enjoy it. I've got to get to work."

Across the water from my office, I noticed the 34-foot boat that's home to my dockmaster, Noah, who works the 3–11 p.m. shift. Plenty of opportunity there. I counted the money in the cash drawer and guessed that someone bought fuel last night, because I'm loaded with twenty-dollar bills. I needed to take them to the front office and exchange them for rolls of quarters. Boaters always need quarters to use the washers and dryers in the lounge, so I must provide change. As I slid the bills into an envelope, I noticed that two of them had identical serial numbers. Actually, three of them did. But the color and texture of the paper looked exceptional. My years in the banking industry blessed me with an amazing grasp of the blatantly obvious—the bills were probably counterfeit.

I called Peter and told him that he needs to call the bank and/or the Secret Service to report it.

"Banks can, at their discretion, replace fake money received by their customers, but they are unlikely to do so," I explained. "It makes very little difference where the counterfeit came from—a store, an individual, or an ATM. In most cases, you'll end up writing off the loss. Banks are in charge of vetting the money that they dispense through their ATMs. If that's where the fake came from, you'll have a better argument for getting a replacement. But my guess is this money didn't come from an ATM."

"The marina is just out of the money?" The anger in Peter's voice was palpable.

"That is a distinct possibility, but why don't you just make that call to be sure?"

A roll of paper towels and a spray bottle of glass cleaner reminded me of the furry shelves that needed my attention. How cat hair floats upward to cover boating brochures and candy bars was beyond my comprehension. But Marina sheds in many more directions than just down to the floor or the chairs. I sprayed and wiped, happy to see immediate results, and one small problem was solved to my satisfaction.

As I put the cleaning tools away, my phone pinged, and I discovered a text from Peter. As usual, it annoyed me. The cold, stripped-down way that people communicate these days frustrated me. I preferred to hear a *voice,* the nuances of meaning detected in a person's *tone.* Better yet,

I wanted to look into their eyes and see an actual *connection.* Texting encouraged miscommunication, something that Peter excelled in.

My shift was almost over, so I called Harri to see if I needed to pick up anything from the grocery store on my way home. She answered on the fourth ring.

"Sorry, I was in the shower."

"In that case, I should make this a video call."

Harri laughed. Actually, it was more of a snort. Only Harri could snort with such elegance.

"I'm getting ready to head home and wondered if you needed anything."

"Just your company."

I grinned into the phone. "See you shortly."

As I gathered paperwork for the next shift to review, my office door swung open. The woman who entered looked vaguely familiar, wearing a glossy blonde bob and a bright Lillie Pulitzer print dress. Her feet were thrust into expensive-looking sandals with heels that would be treacherous on most boat decks as well as my docks.

"Mr. McCracken? We've met before, but you might not remember me. I'm Joan Raffo. My husband, Alberto, and I own the boat that was destroyed in a fire the other night."

"Ah, yes. Nice to see you again, Mrs. Raffo, although not under these circumstances. That was such a terrible incident. The staff at Moss Creek Marina is so sorry about the loss of *Feelin' Nauti.* Unfortunately, I'm afraid the police haven't really given us much information."

"We haven't been told very much either." She gave me a rueful smile. "They said that it's still an active investigation. I wanted to stop in and cancel our dockage agreement, since we no longer have a boat to store here. I'll be happy to pay any outstanding balance, of course. Alberto can't bring himself to come back to the marina just yet. He's too upset. He loved that sailboat."

"I'm sure Peter will have the business office calculate any remaining charges and send you an invoice." I kept my tone solicitous because I couldn't imagine all of the legalities she's had to deal with.

"Did you know that Peter was the one who convinced Alberto to buy a sailboat? I never wanted one, and I really never enjoyed sailing it. As it happens, I love fishing, so I wanted to buy a powerboat. Nothing too large or too showy, but big enough to hold a small head with some decent horsepower to run offshore. Alberto overruled me. But maybe next time, he'll listen."

I smiled at her. "Fishing is a great way to enjoy nature and get away from the demands of life, especially for a busy doctor like your husband. I bet you'll be able to convince him to try it."

She stared at the large yachts docked outside my

office window for a moment before turning to flash a quick smile at me.

"I really do hope you're right, Mr. McCracken. Please feel free to suggest it to my husband when you see him again."

CHAPTER 6

The next morning, Marina met me in the parking lot and *meowed* while leading the way to my office. She often lectured me before I started my shift at seven, and after spending the night prowling the docks in search of lizards and mice, she followed me inside. Like me, she enjoys a hearty breakfast, so I filled her dish with dry kibble before I started the coffee. While she ate, I checked to be sure the hand-held spotlight, VHF radio, and phone had been charged after the night shift and were ready for use.

Pale swirls of pink and blue—nursery colors—illuminated the sky. I stood on the dock for a moment and sipped my coffee from today's cheery *Minions* mug, listening to the clinks of the "Clean Marina" and American flags flying on top of the yardarm. The peacefulness of early morning by the water was one of the reasons I loved my job. The sound of waves lapping at the pilings beneath my feet, accompanied by a soft breeze off the Atlantic were my form of meditation, my refuge.

It was a vastly different experience from running five hundred bank branches in multiple states for large financial institutions. There had been too many mergers and acquisitions to count, too many reductions in staff, until, one day, my own position as a senior vice president was eliminated. A friend alerted me to the open harbormaster job at Moss Creek Marina, and as a lifelong boater (who still needed health insurance coverage), my second career on the docks seemed like a perfect fit.

Tom McDonald arrived at my office shortly after I did. He stood and watched as I removed Marina's hair from the furniture, along with a few tufts floating around the floor. A lint roller turns into a surprisingly satisfying little power tool when you're dealing with a chair that's been claimed by a cat. I pressed the sticky surface against the fabric and dragged it firmly across the seat. The first pass usually fills up fast—cat hair clings to the adhesive in thick, fuzzy layers, almost like you're peeling the chair's winter coat off. As I rolled, I heard that soft, tacky sound of the sheet grabbing every loose strand. When the roller started to lose its stickiness, I peeled away the used layer with a quick rip and kept going. It was a strangely gratifying rhythm: roll, lift, peel, repeat.

"Help yourself to some coffee." I paused and hoisted my own cup in a salute.

"Thanks, buddy. Your coffee is better than my

ex-wife's. Actually, your company is too. Have you found any more funny money in your cash drawer?"

I shook my head and dropped a bite of powdered donut into Marina's dish.

"I've heard a lot of phony hundred-dollar bills have been turning up in South Florida. They're the most popular bill being counterfeited overseas, but here in the United States, it's usually the $20 bill."

Tom added enough powdered cream to his cup to clog my *own* arteries, as well as his.

"Around the holiday season is when the most counterfeit bills start floating around. The Secret Service said in our area, they recover about $5,000 to $6,000 a week, and while that sounds like a lot, the agent I spoke with said it's actually a small amount compared to other parts of the country."

"I feel blessed."

"You should. I've met your wife."

He left, laughing, and I tackled the glass shelves along the marina office wall. In between the travel-size deodorants, toothpaste, toothbrushes, and sunscreen that boaters often run out of was a layer of dust and cat hair that I can literally write my name in. I wondered why none of the other dockmasters—particularly the ones who worked the quiet night shifts—ever considered doing the same.

"I have employed a staff of slobs," I said to no one

but myself.

"You have my sympathies."

The deep voice startled me, and I turned to see a man who looked like he might be the lead dancer for Chippendales standing behind me. He was stuffed into a polyester jacket and a collared shirt that strained at the buttons. I didn't like his hair—too shaved on the sides, too long on the top—or his square jaw. I didn't like his tan, his muscles, or the trendy leather sneakers he had on. And I especially didn't like the badge he waved in my face.

"Detective Joe Squires of the Harbor Cove Police Department. I have a few questions about the boat that burned here recently."

I put down the paper towels.

"I'll be happy to answer them. I'm Baxter McCracken, the harbormaster."

"Were you on duty at the time of the incident?"

"As a matter of fact, I had just started my shift. I'm on duty from 7 a.m. to 3 p.m. Monday through Friday."

"Had you seen anything unusual? Anything out of the ordinary?"

"Truthfully, I hadn't even noticed that the boat wasn't at the dock. The first thing I saw was the explosion."

"Are you acquainted with the owners?" He looked down at his phone. "Dr. Alberto Raffo and his wife, Joan?"

"I have met them, of course. But I never met the

woman who was found inside the cabin. In fact, I had no idea anyone was staying aboard. But I leave the marina during daylight hours, so I wouldn't notice lights on inside the vessel at night."

"The deceased is listed as Miss Nikki Smith, an exotic dancer at Starbutts Men's Club, not too far from here," Squires said. "She worked there most days and some evenings. Apparently, she was a temporary guest of Dr. Raffo aboard the boat. His wife was not pleased when she contacted us to file a restraining order months ago. At this point, we have been unable to find any relatives of Miss Smith and aren't sure if that was even her legal name. Are you sure you have no information regarding the woman? No one in the marina knew her or befriended her?"

He watched me closely, and I found myself trying to remember the last time I'd seen anybody around the *Nauti Buoy*.

"I'm not aware of anyone, but since the boat wasn't tied to the dock directly in front of my office, its occupants were out of my direct line of vision."

Detective Squires looked skeptical but simply shrugged. "Thanks for your help. I'll be in touch."

He paused, possibly debating whether to share additional information. "It looks to be an arson case. Our investigators found an accelerant was used to start the fire. Gasoline."

I watched him march down the dock, heading to the parking lot. I glanced at the cat, curled up in her bed. "That was not a very friendly guy."

Marina didn't even open an eye. She usually paid very little attention to discussions that did not involve food or opening the marina office door. She paid very little attention to this one.

CHAPTER 7

"Do we have any plans for this evening?" I generally check with my lovely wife, who is also my social director, before scheduling anything on my own after work.

"No, darling, but I'm intrigued. What do you have in mind?"

I filled Harri in on my chat with Detective Squires and offered my suggestion. After a lengthy pause, I heard a little laughing sound that ended with "Hmmm . . . am I guaranteed a lovely dinner after? Perhaps a lobster roll?"

"I'll even throw in a bottle of Sancerre for you. I'm on my way."

After a quick shower, I decided to wear a polo shirt, emblazoned with the marina logo to establish my credibility if I needed it.

"I can honestly say I've never been inside a strip club before." Harri slid into the car wearing a tight pair of jeans with a modest blouse and woven leather heels, an outfit that would not look like she was auditioning for a spot on stage. However, it was definitely not a 'schoolmarm' look either.

I feigned shock. "You never had a sorority sister make a little cash on the side in college?"

She turned to give me an icy stare.

The parking lot was fairly full, given that it was only five o'clock. A young woman dressed in a sparkly bra and velvet shorts greeted us at the door and announced the $20 cover charge.

Once inside, it took a few minutes for my eyes to adjust. The club was cloaked in shadows, in stark contrast to the bright Florida sunshine outside. Dim, flickering lights fought against the darkness, casting a murky glow over the small stage. A single spotlight illuminated the young woman swirling around a pole in impossible high heels. Harri and I were escorted to a table closer to the bar than the stage.

"We must not look like big tippers," Harri whispered. "Baxter, my shoes keep sticking to the floor."

"If you think that's bad, wait until you touch the tabletop."

She searched her purse for a disinfectant wipe.

The audience looked like a sparse collection of figures hunched over their drinks, their conversations drowned out by the low thrum of bass-heavy music. A few men sat in the corners, faces half-hidden in shadow, their eyes glinting with a mix of boredom and hunger as they watched the dancer move. Their expressions were inscrutable—I guessed maybe a blend of longing and indifference. It appeared that the performance onstage was as familiar to them as the chipped wooden tables and the aroma of stale cigarettes.

Harri ordered a Coke and requested the can. "I'm not certain about the quality of dishwashing here," she breathed into my ear.

When my beer arrived, I took the bottle and left the glass on the tray.

Just then, a new dancer in a pink sequined bikini took the stage, her movements both graceful and weary. The patrons barely acknowledged her, eyes glazed over, lost in their thoughts or more likely, in the haze of their drinks. Minutes later, the pole dancer who had been onstage when we arrived sauntered up to our table. She was wearing a skirt the size of a cocktail napkin and enough eye makeup to make Tammy Fay Baker cringe.

"Hey there, you two." She smiled. "Did you enjoy the show? I love seeing couples in the audience. Maybe you'd like a private dance?"

She looked coyly at Harri. "I could do both of you."

Harri's smile widened. "I wish you could teach me how to dance in those six-inch stilettos. I'm afraid I'd fall and sprain something. Why don't you sit down and join us?"

I ordered a second beer. "Actually, we're here because of Nikki Smith. She was living in my marina when she died, but she'd invited us to the club to see her perform. I'm sorry we didn't get here sooner."

Her eyes drifted over the logo on my shirt, and she sighed. "Yeah. I still can't believe she's gone. She would never commit suicide, by the way. I don't care what the cops say. They've got it all wrong." She pulled out a vape pen. "I'm Amber."

"Nice to meet you, Amber. I'm Baxter, and this is my wife, Harri. Were you and Nikki good friends?"

"Best friends," she said. "We were *best* friends and we even shared an apartment for a while. I moved in with my boyfriend after the landlord raised our rent, and Nikki found some doctor who let her live on his boat. I don't think he charged her, but we all know there are many ways to pay." She sucked on the device and exhaled.

Harri nodded in sympathy.

"She couldn't afford to pay much rent after she started working the lunch shift here. That was weird because she had a star quality around here, and the customers loved her. All the girls know that the biggest tippers come in at night, but Nikki said she didn't want to work late anymore. And she didn't seem very worried about making less money. Go figure. Maybe she won the lottery."

"Did you speak with her recently?"

"She called once, but I didn't answer. I sleep in most mornings when I work late. I don't know who she met or what she was doing, but it definitely wasn't drugs. I just knew that she didn't have much time to spend with me anymore."

"Did she say anything about having a new boyfriend?"

Amber stared at me before she shook her head and pointed the vape pen at my chest.

"You know what I really think, Baxter? I think Nikki got involved with the wrong people, and something really bad happened. I'm not saying it was the doc, but something definitely changed in her life."

She glanced at the bartender, who stood silently observing us, and stood to leave. Harri and I watched her walk away, wobbling slightly in her high heels.

My wife reached for my hand and squeezed it. "I believe it was a blessing that I never learned to walk in six-inch stilettos. And I also believe that we should call our own daughter in Chicago when we get home."

The night's dampness brought a shiver as we walked to our car in silence.

"Nikki Smith was a young woman of many secrets." Harri clicked her seatbelt slowly.

"Apparently, she no longer needed to earn much of an income, so some*one* or some*thing* was supporting her."

Harri shifted in her seat to face me. "Are you implying

that she was connected to the drugs you found hidden in the boater's lounge?"

"I can't rule it out. Seems like my dockmasters would notice more foot traffic in the marina, though. I need to chat with Tom McDonald. A retired sheriff always has good instincts."

"Good idea, but it can wait until tomorrow. I'm starving and don't want the lobster that the restaurant is boiling for me to die in vain."

CHAPTER 8

Under the intensity of the morning sun, I noticed the ground looked brighter, the colors of the grass and mulch appeared slightly overexposed, and the insect world seemed to hum a little louder. It was an early cue that the day would be hot and that summer was fully awake when I headed to breakfast at my favorite Cuban cafe, wedged in a tiny strip mall near the marina. I caught a whiff of freshly baked bread the moment I opened my car door. Tom arrived as I sipped a scalding hot Café con Leche that threatened to remove the flesh on the roof of my mouth as well as my tongue.

I gestured to the menu, which was written in Spanish and English. "My recommendation is the *Desayuno Criollo*, which includes two fried eggs and two ham croquetas, breaded and fried to golden perfection. It comes with an order of buttered Cuban toast and a nap."

"Sounds perfectly delicious. But you, my friend, must go to work."

Tom didn't ask what I wanted to speak with him about, but I launched into a five-minute rundown of my visit to the strip club, taking a break when the waitress appeared to take his order. There was a dull murmur of conversation all around us. Laborers in denim jeans and paint-splattered overalls mixed with a few people in business attire, seated at the old wooden tables.

"As a live-aboard guest, have you seen any unusual comings or goings at night? It's terrifying to consider, but do you think the dead girl may have been part of a drug ring operating out of our marina?"

Tom added a second packet of sugar to his coffee mug and stirred it slowly.

"I haven't noticed any activity that made me feel uneasy. If I do, you know that I'll head to your office immediately."

I leaned back in my chair and tried to relax.

"Thanks, I appreciate that. The police are hinting at suicide, but her friend didn't agree. She thinks something bad happened to Nikki. But without any known relatives pushing for answers, the police may just close the case. Of course, I would like to know the truth, particularly if someone at my marina was involved."

"If I were still working for the Sheriff's Office, I'd be looking at the doctor boyfriend. Most of the time, the romantic partner is the perpetrator of the crime."

I toasted Tom with my mug and ventured another sip. "At times like this, I wish I'd read more Agatha Christie novels."

"It's faster to just watch the movies," he said. "Trust me, my friend, *real* justice moves at a glacial pace."

With a full stomach and the taste of café con leche lingering on my scorched tongue, I arrived at the dockmaster's office and enjoyed the calm that early mornings bring. My view of the water was a scene that even the Impressionist painters would have envied. As I began reviewing the dockage agreements from the previous night's shift, I spotted a forty-eight-foot Sea Ray approaching my fuel dock faster than it should. I grabbed my hat and headed outside to assist. A middle-aged woman stood at the bow, clutching a line as she looked over her shoulder. The man at the helm was having difficulty bringing his boat parallel to the dock and yelled at her to throw me a line. I didn't like his tone, but I've heard it often enough. When the newly retired no longer have staff to bully, they inevitably turn their wrath toward the only person close by—their spouse.

Forward, then reverse. Forward, then reverse … Unfortunately, many people who have the financial means to *buy* large boats also lack the *skills* to operate them. (Unlike driving a car, operating a powerboat does not require a license.) This guy had no business trying to run a boat that size with his lack of ability. Blaming his wife, who was clearly embarrassed by his angry outbursts and mouthed the word *"Sorry"* to me, only made the situation worse.

But God was merciful, and the frazzled woman finally tossed a line that didn't land in the water and reached me. I smiled at her, swallowed my frustration, and began my basic seamanship instruction to her incompetent husband.

"Captain, now that you have a bowline attached to my piling, put your port engine in reverse at idle, and it will pull the stern back in."

Miraculously, the boat docked, although the man's wife looked as though she was close to tears. After filling his fuel tanks, I retreated to the air-conditioned office and debated which would come first for that unfortunate couple—a divorce or the sale of the Sea Ray.

After a series of uneventful daily rounds, I looked up from my paperwork and saw Angela arriving for her shift.

"Hey, Cap'n Mac. How's it going today?"

"Blessedly quiet, actually."

She grinned. "I think you might be looking for another dockmaster to help out."

I'm confused, since the ambulance chaser recently hired a twenty-five-year-old army reservist whose previous marina experience was limited to teaching sailing classes to young teens at a yacht club in the area. When the kid shadowed me for a couple of days, he appeared to be intelligent, and I thought he had potential. Unfortunately, while he was always respectful to me, Angela described his behavior toward her—and any other female he encountered—as very dismissive of women.

"Angela, please tell me that you're not leaving Moss Creek Marina."

When she laughed and shook her head, I continued. "Clearly, I've missed something. Tell me what's happened."

Angela described starting her shift and logging into the Daily Operating Report (DOR) as well as checking the marina emails. "I noticed tons of Google searches—online job searches—on our marina computer," she said. "Plus, there were almost as many dating websites as job sites that were logged into."

When she picked up the marina cell phone (every dockmaster on duty carries the marina cell phone with them during rounds) Angela also discovered lots of outgoing, lengthy calls to long-distance area codes, which is unusual for a small, historic marina in Florida. Yacht owners or their captains call the marina during normal business hours rather than late at night.

"That may explain why we've been going through print cartridges and paper a lot faster than usual," I said. "The kid probably doesn't own a computer at his apartment and is obviously unaware that the public library has them available to use for free. Looks like he's been job hunting while he's supposed to be working *here*."

"Wait, it gets better," she giggled. "When Noah came on duty at 11 p.m., he told me that he found the guy making out with a woman in our office. Other nights, when he's had too much to drink at the bar next door, Noah said he crashes on the couch in here to sleep it off."

Admittedly, it was difficult to hire competent staff to work at a marina that remained open twenty-four hours a day. Not long ago, I suffered through another of Peter's hasty hires: a fifty-something man who had been recommended by one of Peter's country club friends—probably someone who had represented the idiot in court. That particular candidate arrived for his dockmaster training carrying a 38-caliber pistol in his pocket.

"If anyone messes with me, I shoot first and ask questions later," he assured me.

"Unfortunately, the owner of this marina won't let you carry a weapon of any sort while you are on site," I replied.

A workplace that involves boats, customers, fuel docks, and closequarters teamwork already has its own stresses. Adding a firearm to that environment could disastrously amplify emotions, which I had no desire to deal with.

Later, when I informed Peter of the issue, he had a

predictable meltdown over his liability and dismissed the man immediately. Private employers in Florida are legally allowed to ban firearms inside their buildings and work areas. Even though Florida allows concealed carry in many *public* spaces, workplaces are treated differently because they are private property, and owners like Peter can set safety policies for their employees. His reaction was a great relief to me.

I prefer working with *fewer* employees rather than *foolish* ones.

CHAPTER 9

THE AMBULANCE CHASER SCHEDULED AN 8 a.m. Safety Meeting, stating attendance was mandatory for all employees. When it came to the marina business, Peter rarely asked opinions or took polls. In truth, dockmasters don't have to be licensed to do their job. Anybody with knowledge of boating qualifies—a true yet dangerous loophole. Safety meetings are really designed for people working in high-risk situations, like scraping the bottom of a sixty-foot yacht while it rests on wooden blocks in the boatyard. They're also necessary to meet insurance liability policies. If an accident *does* happen, the marina owner must show that he provided adequate safety training to his workers.

The air was crisp, but the sun was already strong when I arrived at the front office, carrying my own coffee because previous experience taught me that Peter would not provide any beverages for his employees, and I surveyed the room. Only half of the current employees even bothered to show up: three from the dockmaster's office, three from the boatyard, and the office secretary.

"I know that you all understand the importance of safety, but I have to hold these meetings twice a year to get a 10 percent discount on my casualty insurance. I know that you all know how to do your jobs, but let me give you one piece of advice—don't try to do your job while standing on one leg."

A bit of forced laughter. I took a deep breath followed by a sip of my coffee. It was clear that Peter didn't take this seriously, and as a result, no one else would either. From Peter's point of view, saving money was more important than saving lives. I decided it might be helpful to actually offer a *real* safety tip.

"On a serious note, folks, we tie up boats every day. I caution everyone never to let their fingers get between a dock line and a piling. Remember, that's an easy way to lose a finger."

Heads nodded in agreement to the sole moment of value that occurred during the meeting. A worker from the boatyard mustered the courage to offer a second safety tip regarding power tools, and with that, the meeting ended. There was no mention of the travel lift hoisting a boat out of the water and accidentally ripping the bow rail off of another vessel because of an untrained "spotter" standing by. Who needs a safety meeting?

The heat was already deadly outside as I walked back

to my office. The sun had been baking the dock planks since dawn, and Captain Karen was waiting for me aboard her 128-foot motor yacht. "Hey, I'm heading out later for a lunch cruise, and I need a bit of fuel."

My diesel dispenser delivers sixteen-and-a-half gallons per minute, so filling her 1,000-gallon tank would take about an hour. I hooked up the hose to her boat, and she monitored the gauges down in her engine room. I remained on the dock, checking every six minutes to be sure there were no clogs in the fuel line while it was pumping.

After charging $4,000 to the captain's black AMEX, I headed out to check on an elderly couple who were staying aboard their vintage Huckins yacht while slowly working their way back North. I'd had a call on Saturday from one of my dockmasters on duty to report that the Huckins had no power. I asked if they had checked the breaker—they had—and it was working. Of course, the ambulance chaser has refused to call an electrician due to the higher weekend rates. He insisted it was the boat's problem, not the marinas. Since I hadn't heard anything more, I assumed the problem had been resolved. But as I approached the beautiful old yacht, I saw both husband and wife loading black plastic trash bags with spoiled food from their refrigerator. Clearly, they still had no power.

"We just can't seem to figure this out," the husband said, wiping his face on his sleeve.

I assured him that I would discover the cause and repair it before I hoisted two of the trash bags and headed to the dumpster. Their power cord was plugged into the shore power box mounted on our wooden dock. My first call went straight to Peter's voicemail. My second call went to an electrician the marina has on call. Within an hour, I learned the power lines that run under the dock somehow had been severed.

"Of course, the marina will reimburse you for the food that spoiled when your power went out," I told our guests. I imagined that Peter would be thrilled to write that check.

"Our friends told us that you were the best harbormaster on the East Coast," he said, shaking my hand. "I see they were right."

On the way back to my office, I noticed Noah entertaining guests, displaying a lot of leather clothes and a lot of tattoos. It looked like a small biker convention. I watched them bro-hug, one arm apiece, each slapping the other man's back as if to dislodge an obstruction in his throat. I couldn't be sure, but I thought several of them seemed jittery as I passed the boat. Noah merely raised his hand and waved. "Morning, Cap'n Mac."

I waved and kept walking.

The steady migration of boats from South Florida—where marinas are overcrowded and terribly expensive—increased demand in Central Florida for slips that can accommodate larger vessels. Today, dredges are as common as seagulls along the coast. At Moss Creek Marina, silt builds up, so we need to be sure that bigger boats don't sit on the harbor bottom at low tide.

The marina owns six barges, roughly twenty by forty feet. Each barge has two "spuds" (hollow steel pilings), which hook up to a crane that picks them up from the seabed and drops them in place. Peter planned to dredge it down to eight feet at low tide so bigger boats could dock. A second barge was needed alongside the first, so the crane could deposit all of the muck it pulled up. Finally, an aluminum push boat with two 150-horsepower Suzuki outboard engines moved the barge back to shore, where a second crane offloaded the muck onto dry land at the south end of the marina. It was left to dry in the sun before Peter sold it as fill dirt for local construction sites.

But whispers from the boatyard indicated that a disgruntled customer threatened to report Peter to the EPA for failing to obtain the proper permits. Dredging spoil and selling it as fill dirt requires permits because the stuff can be loaded with toxic contaminants like pesticides and heavy metals. Those pose a risk to water quality, wildlife, and human health if they're just dumped as fill. The permitting process ensured the material was tested and that the impact on the environment would be minimal. I never questioned my boss's possible illicit dumping and didn't speak of it around my dockmasters. Still, I wondered how many folks who had been antagonized by Peter might be motivated to cause legal trouble for his marina.

In the meantime, Peter loved to play with his heavy equipment, so I frequently ferried him and a deckhand out to the barge. On those days, he traded his expensive lawyer suit for a T-shirt and shorts to run the crane. That meant my regular duties were constantly interrupted to take 5-gallon jugs of diesel to run the crane, plus gasoline to power the bilge pump. The barge seemed to continuously take on water and relied on portable pumps to prevent it from sinking. Overnight rain caused more problems, including a surly response from Peter if the weather denied him an opportunity to amuse himself on the barge.

On difficult days, I tried to remember my wife's astute armchair analysis: "There are happy, well-adjusted people out there. People whose lives have meaning and purpose, who have weathered life's blows and come out stronger and wiser. They just don't work for Moss Creek Marina."

CHAPTER 10

FLORIDA SEASONS ARE MEASURED WITH a rain gauge more than with a thermometer. One of my daily tasks—as a harbormaster as well as a native Floridian—was to check the National Oceanic and Atmospheric Administration (NOAA) website daily. During the Atlantic hurricane season, I paid particular attention to tropical cyclone activity in the Caribbean. I always wanted to be well ahead of the curve if a storm was coming. This morning, I listened to the National Hurricane Center issue advisories for the eastern seaboard as I poured my Cheerios into a bowl. A handful of local boat owners who live on the water pay an annual fee to reserve a spot in our sheltered marina—either in the water or on the hard—in the event of a named storm. A backyard dock that's exposed to rough seas and high winds will destroy any vessel tied to it.

If their vessel is small enough, some owners elect to move it further inland to protected waters. Larger yachts have to make their best guess whether to stay in my marina or move either north or south of where the storm is expected to hit. We give priority to our current year-round customers. Ten percent of our customers take their boats north before hurricane season starts on June first because some insurance policies won't cover a vessel if it's left in the path of a hurricane (unless you have specifically bought coverage). If we have any additional space available, we offer it on a first-come, first-served basis to boat owners who call the marina and request it.

"Remember the category five storm that was supposed to hit us a few years ago?" Harri emerged from our bedroom in walking gear, ready for her morning cardio workout. "When the governor announced, 'If you don't leave now, it will be too late', thousands of residents clogged the interstate highways only to be trapped in traffic because there wasn't a single empty hotel room from Miami to Charleston. Even worse—but better for Floridians, of course—the hurricane turned into the Atlantic Ocean and missed its projected landfall. Call me an optimist, but I don't think we should start yelling 'The sky is falling' just yet."

She grabbed a carton of half and half and poured a splash into her coffee, watching it swirl in circles before it dispersed. I knew this was her favorite part of the day, and I welcomed her company at the breakfast table.

"I totally agree with you, but don't tell me that you don't relish spending soggy, sleepless nights watching Jim

Cantore and the rest of the meteorologists at The Weather Channel pelted with rain."

"It's just like you to look for the silver lining, my dear." She smiled.

By the time I reached my office, my phone was lighting up like a pinball machine. Our location was predicted to be in the path of the potential storm, so the deluge of people asking for a safe location to bring their boats would continue. Standing on the dock, I enjoyed the warm breeze but not the view. Gone were the shimmering waves and storybook clouds. Today the water lifted its jaws to bite, foaming at the mouth. Even the sky looked like a battleship—gray with a deep blue stripe at its center. I noticed Peter's son standing on the far dock, his eyes focused on the drone flying above his head. For a moment, I wondered if lightning ever struck drones. If it did, that would certainly add to my current problems, but I decided to focus on the ones that I could solve.

I already emailed all of our current customers, reminding them about hurricane preparation. I recommended they come to their vessel and upgrade the dock lines with larger lines, reduce windage by removing sail covers or Bimini tops, and lash down everything that couldn't be removed. They needed to make sure their batteries were charged and their bilge pumps were working. It was also a good idea to top off the fuel tanks to prevent any water absorption and empty any food from the refrigerator on board. If the owners lived too far away, they generally hired the marina staff to do it for them.

Apparently, his caseload was down because Peter focused all of his attention on instructing me how to do my job. I guessed it stemmed from his fear that damage to the marina might force him to shut down. If the boatyard closed, it couldn't produce revenue, so he repeatedly told me what needed to be done. Of course, in most cases, I'd already done it.

Marina prowled the office, unsure if she wanted to remain inside or out. The cat's instincts were good. Outside, she would be vulnerable to strong winds, falling debris, and flooding if the storm hit. I scratched her ears, and she meowed her gratitude. Birds and marine animals also sense changes in air pressure and move to higher ground or deeper water. Many birds fly inland well before a hurricane makes landfall. Humans could learn a lot from them, especially those who live in waterfront condos.

I poured my coffee into a *Lucky Irish* mug that must have been left behind by some crew on Saint Patrick's Day. Gordon stopped in, carrying a warm guava pastry with an aroma that promised my day would get better.

"Morning, Cap'n Mac. I figured I'd better get this pastry to you before the little cafe shuts down for the storm. Then again, if the wind is strong enough, it might blow us a few pastries all the way from Cuba."

"A delightful thought, my friend. What's happening in the boatyard?"

"We're working on the 'hurricane haul out' list, our customers who have reserved a space on land and paid us in advance," Gordon said. "We've already blocked three boats this morning."

I've watched as workers picked up a boat with the travel lift and lowered it onto a group of wooden blocks, similar to railroad ties. The hull rested straight and level above ground, with the blocks strategically placed to avoid the keel, rudder, and propeller. Depending on the size of the boat, added jack stands (two at the stern, two midships, and two at the bow) prevented the vessel from tipping over in strong winds.

"I haven't run out of dock space yet, but I'm getting close. My phone won't stop ringing with anxious boat owners."

During hurricane season, if we run out of linear feet of dock, with the owner's permission, we'll raft a second boat to one that's currently docked and separate the vessels using inflatable fenders. When boats are tied tightly together, they rise and fall on the tide in tandem to avoid any damage to either vessel.

As he waved goodbye, Gordon nearly collided with Noah, who was reaching for my office door. I was surprised to see him in advance of his shift and even more surprised when he announced his departure ahead of the storm. "We're sailing north to Jacksonville, where my wife has a job at a new bank. We found a spot to keep the boat, but the storm predictions have sped up our plans. We'd like to go before the weather gets bad and the rain starts. Stay safe, Cap'n Mac."

I wished him well and felt strangely relieved. Contrary to Noah's report, the pest control guy hadn't found any bedbugs in the boater's lounge. It occurred to me that rumors regarding an infestation of insects wasn't a bad way to keep people out of a place and away from those plastic bags filled with white powder. I hadn't discovered any more since the burning boat incident, which also made me wonder if Nikki Smith was involved. A nagging voice inside my head debated whether she was somehow connected to Noah. Fortunately, the increased police patrols at night provided a visual deterrent to drug deals, but the guests aboard Noah's boat had frequently concerned me. They reminded me of insect bites: even though you're determined not to scratch, they were nevertheless a source of irritation.

Noah's departure left me with only two remaining liveaboards: my friend, Tom McDonald, and an older woman named Linda, who resided in a twenty-six-foot Columbia sailboat that was not plugged into shore power. I saw her many days shortly after I arrived in the morning, leaving the ladies' restroom and shower facilities. Her daily wardrobe consisted of sun-protective shirts with the sleeves rolled at the elbows and cargo shorts. Linda's skin matched the color and texture of the Sperry leather boat shoes she wore on her feet. On rare occasions, I noticed her wearing lipstick. Rumor had it she was divorced, but no known relatives were listed on her dockage agreement. We had no one to contact in case of an accident.

She rode a bicycle to the library every day and frequently returned with one or two canvas grocery bags dangling from the handlebars. I marveled at how she survived daily life in the Florida heat using only an ice chest and a camp stove. She mentioned that she once worked for the Central Florida Zoo, but what she specifically did there remained a mystery. For some, living on a boat offered the potential for travel. Linda, however, never left the dock.

My best guess was that she appreciated the affordable alternative to renting or owning a house on land. Some liveaboards were drawn to the idea of living with fewer possessions, which the limited space on a boat encouraged.

Then again, the daily experience of waking up to the water and being surrounded by nature continued to be a significant draw. The liveaboard lifestyle required a degree of resourcefulness combined with a willingness to adapt to the unique demands of living on a boat that required ongoing maintenance.

Linda appeared very intelligent and frequently brought me articles that she'd cut out of newspapers or magazines regarding ecology, religion, and global warming. On her way to or from the showers, she would stop by my office and plop something on my desk with the comment, "Thought you might want to read this."

Daily interactions with neighbors on the docks, like this, fostered a greater sense of community than in many traditional neighborhoods, including my own. More importantly, liveaboards acted as my eyes and ears: Residents often alerted my dockmasters to issues like leaks, intruders, or maintenance needs. They acted as informal stewards of the marina, people who cared about it as much as I did.

Marina wasn't the only animal that sensed trouble in the air. My boss appeared particularly agitated as he watched the weather and storm reports. Ever the optimist, I thought a bit of good news might improve his darkening mood.

"You know, Peter, I just have to tell you that your daughter, Angela, does a great job for me. It's refreshing to see someone so young with such a terrific work ethic."

Peter scratched his head and shrugged. "Yeah, she's always been like that. Angela never played dress up or had tea parties—not even when she was small. She was outside organizing soccer games with the boys, climbing trees, or playing hide-and-seek. That kid was always motivated to accomplish things. She never whined about being bored."

He left to direct storm preparations in the boatyard shortly before Angela arrived for her shift. Smiling, she shyly pointed to a few matted photographs of boats that she recently hung on the wall. "I hope you don't mind that I put those up Cap'n Mac. I used pushpins to anchor them because we didn't have a hammer or nails."

"Angela, I'm delighted that you did. Our office looks so much better with a gallery of art. Thank you for thinking of it."

"It gave me something to do when it got quiet during my shift last night," she said. "Hey, I've been meaning to ask you, uh, if you heard any more from the police about the doctor's boat that burned? My dad refuses to talk about it, and my mom . . . Well, you've met her. She doesn't like to discuss unpleasant things at the dinner table."

"I understand. Your father also wants to avoid any

scandal for the marina, which is understandable. But secrets only protect reputations temporarily. I think the potential storm may have slowed the police investigation. But I promise I'll share updates with you whenever I receive them."

CHAPTER 11

As I PEELED A RIPE banana at my kitchen window, the sun burst from behind the clouds, making the possibility of an approaching hurricane look ridiculous. Before the invention of Doppler radar, Florida's pioneer residents would never have suspected that a storm might be coming. Harri stood behind me and perched her chin on my shoulder. She smelled of lavender soap and shampoo.

"This morning appears to be, quite literally, the calm before the storm."

I offered her a bite of a banana. "Have some potassium, my dear. You'll need your strength if the weather worsens."

She hugged me as she chewed. "Have you considered a second career as a nutritionist? No one could possibly resist your advice."

Nodding, I dropped two slices of sourdough into the toaster and waited.

"Next time I need a change of career, I promise I'll

consider it. In the meantime, I suggest that we stop and buy a case of bottled water today before the grocery stores run out of it. My suggestion is made simply out of an abundance of caution, of course."

"No problem. I'll get it after I meet with my editor this morning. And I've stocked the pantry with our favorite water crackers, smoked oysters, tuna fish, peanut butter, and jelly. We can survive Armageddon if we have to."

"Your efficiency continues to amaze me. I believe the Red Cross only recommends a three-day supply of non-perishable food items."

"I hope I'll continue to exceed your expectations." She gave me a bawdy wink.

My wife knows my body as well as she knows the can opener in our kitchen drawer. She's had both since college. Wrapping my arms around her, I planted a kiss. "Let me assure you that I didn't marry you for your expertise in the kitchen."

I gathered my sunscreen, my Swiss Army knife, an electrolyte drink, and my wide-brimmed hat before I headed to the marina. My office was fragrant with the scent of freshly brewed coffee and clean mugs—hand-washed by the overnight dockmaster—beckoned from a drying rack next to the sink. I selected one emblazoned with dancing skeletons that said, *Happy Halloween,* and tackled a pile of overnight paperwork that Daniel, my boss's son, left on the counter at the end of his shift.

An hour later, I looked up to see Dr. Raffo approaching the marina office, impeccably dressed in a linen sport coat adorned with a colorful pocket square and a large gold signet ring that glinted on his little finger. It was hardly standard marina attire for boaters, so I guessed that he had come to view the remnants of his sailboat in the yard. I told him how sorry I was about the loss.

"Yeah, well, it's only money, right?" Then, as if catching himself in the callousness of his response, he added, "I mean, it's terrible about the loss of life, too. That poor girl, uh, Nikki Smith."

The nonchalant way he referred to the dead young woman shocked me. How could a medical doctor be as indifferent to the end of a life as he was to a weather forecast?

I did not comment but simply asked if the police had made any headway on the case, and he shrugged. "Not really. I just know that I'm not at fault. They told me thousands of young adults die each year, and law enforcement frequently can't find any family members to contact. The cause of death varies—drug overdoses, homicide, suicide—those statistics increased significantly over the last five years. Young people seem to be more vulnerable to substance abuse and risky behaviors, I guess."

His description of Nikki didn't match what I'd heard

from her friend at the strip joint. She described Nikki as a focused young woman who preferred to dance during the lunch shift and wasn't into drugs. Her friend didn't believe she would ever commit suicide either. That meant the man standing in front of me either was lying or he didn't know the young lady very well.

Dr. Raffo was silent for a moment, but when he spoke again, his voice was quiet. "When you reach my age, there are many moments—many decisions—that you wish you could go back and make again. Choose a different path. Allowing Nikki Smith to stay aboard that sailboat is one of mine."

It was a relief when he headed to the boatyard, and I turned my attention to a 43-foot Wellcraft San Remo double-cabin motor yacht that was delinquent on three months of dockage. According to his attorney, the owner was involved in an accident in Italy that resulted in two broken legs. After numerous texts, emails, and phone calls, I'd been assured of at least a partial payment. In addition, I reminded the attorney that my next step was a non-judicial sale of the vessel. That means a marina holding a lien on a yacht for unpaid services can sell it without a court order to recover the money. The process involved providing the owner with proper written notice and an itemized invoice of the charges owed, followed by a public advertisement of the sale at a specific time and place. I hoped it wouldn't come to that, but the documents were already prepared.

Glancing at the clock, I noticed it was time to make my rounds. A walk would clear my head, and I always enjoyed seeing dock lines and fenders in the right position. Marina followed me for part of the way but veered off to chase a lizard. By the time I reached the boatyard, I was surprised to see *Ed's Mobile Marine* van parked next to my final dock. Ed was a fine marine mechanic who drove a Ford Econoline loaded with parts and supplies. Large boats couldn't travel to *him*, so when problems with a system on board arose, Ed traveled to the boat. Yet I vaguely remembered hearing about a disagreement between him and Peter that resulted in Ed being banned from Moss Point Marina. That memory was confirmed when I saw Peter sprinting toward the dock, yelling, "You've got to get out of that boat. You're not allowed in this marina."

Ed emerged from below deck on the vessel where he was working and turned to face Peter. I was too far away to hear what was said, but even wearing Polarized sunglasses, I saw the boss's face turn an interesting shade of crimson as he shouted, "Really? You wanna fight?"

Peter planted his feet in a boxer stance, and that's when I decided to pivot on mine. A fistfight? Really? Though not unexpected, his antagonistic behavior had plummeted to a new low, and I couldn't bear to witness any more of it.

CHAPTER 12

THE WEATHER OUTSIDE PROVIDED A soundtrack of rain tapping on the windows when I got home. Harri reclined on the sofa, watching The Weather Channel. As I bent to greet her, a young meteorologist proclaimed that the storm had weakened, moved east-northeast, and was aimed directly at Bermuda. Despite feeling relieved, I knew that the wind, rain, massive waves, and a dangerous storm surge—all remnants of the storm—still would be felt up and down the East Coast, including at my marina.

"Darling, I think we've dodged a bullet." Harri patted my back. "To celebrate, I marinated a pork tenderloin in olive oil, soy sauce, garlic, and Dijon honey mustard. It's waiting for your expert hands to cook it on the grill."

"Sounds amazing. To be honest, I don't remember stopping to eat lunch today, and I'm ravenous. But the grill master needs five minutes for a shower."

A cascade of hot water massaged my skin as I watched thick steam cloud the glass shower door and mirrors. The small enclosure transformed into a private, misty sanctuary where I could fold my arms and think. Something about Dr. Raffo's description of the death of a young woman aboard his sailboat seemed callous and remote. He definitely did not sound like a man who was upset by the loss of his young lover in a tragic accident. Nor did he sound like a murderer. Why quote statistics about young adult deaths? Something didn't add up. The constant drumming of water against the tile floor helped wash away my mental debris.

Later, as I sliced the tenderloin, I shared my observations with Harri. She agreed that Dr. Raffo's response seemed odd.

"Don't you remember that both the good doctor and his wife took out restraining orders on poor Nikki? That tells me there was some sort of problem going on. Perhaps he seemed detached to you because he was afraid to appear too involved."

"Oh, it's 'poor Nikki' now?"

Harri waved a slice of avocado on the end of her fork. "I just remembered our visit to Starbutts Men's Club, that dreadful strip joint where she worked. Such a sad place, but her friend believed she was healthy and *happy,* not a drug-addled, suicide risk. She was probably close to our own daughter's age, and that girl had her whole life looming ahead of her until . . . one day, she didn't."

Harri walked to the refrigerator and opened the door

as though searching for answers. When she couldn't find any, she opened another bottle of Sancerre.

"We're missing something or *someone,*" I declared as I rinsed my plate. "Peter's code of silence isn't helping anyone find the truth either."

She shooed me out of the kitchen and sent me to the back porch, where palm trees rustled above my head in the damp air. The neighbors' wind chimes played a solemn tune in accompaniment. My watch indicated it was seven o'clock, and I decided I could spare a little time to relax without checking my emails. The rain had stopped, and the sun was sinking in a blaze of red, orange, and lavender. I was aware, on some level of consciousness, that this would be a good thing for me to be doing. Relaxation came easily whenever I spent time outdoors.

I still watched every sunset, hoping to see the "green flash," although I am grateful to be among the fortunate few who have witnessed the rare optical phenomenon. It happened only once: Harri and I dropped our son off at a marina on Boca Grande to pick up his car and return to the University of Miami following spring break. As we motored our rental boat slowly back to Useppa Island, we turned to watch the sunset. At that moment, we saw a tiny but brilliant green spot where the last ray of the upper rim of the sun hung on the horizon. It lasted no more than two seconds and resembled the puff of smoke that rises when a candle is extinguished. Harri and I turned to each other in disbelief and simultaneously asked, "Did you see that?"

I later learned that clear, unobstructed views over the Gulf of Mexico provide the clear skies and flat horizon that's necessary to see the fleeting spectacle. For the green light to appear, the atmosphere must be exceptionally stable and free of haze. Florida's coastal areas have ideal conditions, sometimes enhanced by a layer of cool air below warmer air, which acts like a magnifying lens. Florida residents—especially on the west coast and in the Florida Keys—routinely watch for the "green flash," and consider it a "bucket list" item. While many tourists dismiss it as a myth, I have assured anyone who asks me that it is *not*.

Harri juggled two cups of Cafe Bustelo, topped with the perfect amount of steamed froth. "I forgot to mention that I googled Dr. Alberto Raffo, and it turns out he's had two malpractice suits filed against him in recent years. Another involved dealing in pain medications." Her face beamed as she added, "Guess who always represented him?"

"Peter Johnson?"

"Bravo. You are such a clever man."

"Who won the cases?"

"Dr. Raffo prevailed, although I'm not sure if that's due to his innocence or to Peter's skill as a litigator. Wait, there's more."

Harri lunged for her phone, and her eyes darted

across the screen, swiping and tapping with increasing urgency. Her brows knit together, her lips slightly parted as she muttered to herself, "Where is it? I know I took a screenshot." The glow of the phone illuminated her face, revealing a flush of frustration as she scrolled through albums. I knew better than to interrupt, so I sipped my coffee and watched as notifications popped up, distracting her, but she dismissed them with a sharp flick. She paused, eyes scanning the screen for a clue. Then—finally—she held up the phone triumphantly, the elusive photo shimmering on its screen. "Do you recognize anyone?"

Leaning in, I saw an old newspaper picture of a man who looked like an impossibly young Peter Johnson. Standing beside him appeared to be an equally young version of Joan Raffo.

"Is that . . ."

"You betcha. Her hair is quite a bit longer, and she's identified in the cutline by her maiden name. But the article heralds Peter Johnson's acceptance into a rather prestigious law school. It seems that Joan Raffo and your favorite counselor were once an item in college."

I stared at my wife. "Imagine that."

Overnight, I received a text message that one of our channel markers had been hit by a passing vessel, so in the morning, I hopped into my 20-foot center console boat to check for damage. The sun was already soaking through my shirt and settling into my muscles as I idled past the third set of pilings. A blonde woman waved from her Gheenoe, a 16-foot cross between a canoe and a flats boat that only drew five inches of water. The shallow draft allowed access to areas that would be inaccessible to larger boats. In addition, their quiet operation was ideal for stealthy approaches to fish, although it had an electric motor on the bow for trolling. It was advertised as a versatile, lightweight, and stable boat primarily used for fishing, which is why I was surprised to recognize Joan Raffo steering the vessel with a paddle.

"Good morning, Cap'n Mac. Isn't this a perfectly beautiful morning to be on the water?"

She pulled alongside my boat, grabbed the rail, and gestured toward her Gheenoe. "What do you think of my new guilty pleasure? It was a present from me to myself. Some evenings I go out alone to fish the tides. I find a lot of snook in the shallows. Alberto never cared much for fishing, I'm afraid."

I smiled. "Hey, that just means more fish stories for you to tell—and maybe one day, he'll realize what he's been missing."

The sides of her mouth turned downward as Joan lowered her eyes. "I really do hope that you're right. I'd like that."

When I got back to the dock, I heard Marina from the dense tangle of bushes at the edge of the yard—a sound so mournful it seemed to vibrate through the air like a siren. The cat's cry rose and fell in eerie waves, a banshee's wail wrapped in a fur coat. Crouching low, I crept toward the source, parting branches. Two glowing eyes blinked from the shadows, and Marina, fur bristling and tail puffed like a bottlebrush, stood hunched over something unseen. Small things can be hidden in public places, so I reached out, whispered some soothing nonsense, and slowly pulled a muddy cell phone from the bushes. The case originally appeared to be covered in purple glitter, with a faint letter "N" printed in the middle. My heart gave an extra thump.

Immediately, I headed for Tom McDonald's boat, hoping that he knew someone who specialized in digital forensics and could recover data from a soggy, mud-covered phone. I found him aboard, unpacking groceries in the galley.

"I do know someone, but don't you want to turn this in to the police? It may contain crucial evidence."

"Of course I intend to, but I'd like to learn something first, if that's even possible. Technically, we don't know for certain that this phone even belonged to the dead girl."

He sighed. "I think this is an idiotic idea, but I'll agree to make a phone call. My friend probably can check to see if the phone was synced to iCloud, or Google Drive or OneDrive, if it's an Android," he explained. "Those backups may contain photos, messages, and contacts. If I remember this correctly, the success rate depends on removing the SIM card gently and letting it air dry. Just don't try to turn the phone on, charge it, or press any buttons. I mean, it's worth a shot if my friend can get to it quickly. But if he's backlogged or there's any sort of delay, promise me that you'll hand it in to the police and beg for their results."

I agreed to his terms and waited in a deck chair, gently wiping the phone with a microfiber cloth while Tom went below to make the call.

"My friend says recovering data from a cell phone that's had mud or water damage can be extremely challenging because mud is abrasive and corrosive," he said when he returned. "He warned me not to use heat like a hairdryer or an oven, because that might cause further damage. His last order was to keep it powered off and dry until he gets here."

Three hours later, a young man who barely looked old enough to own a driver's license stood in my office and informed me that it might take a few days for him to open the phone, clean the logic board with isopropyl alcohol, and repair the damaged components inside.

"I'll probably have to use some specialized tools like vacuum chambers to remove any liquid or debris that was left behind and access data directly from the storage chip," he said. "Many people think they're supposed to put the phone in rice, which is totally ineffective and can even cause mold or corrosion. It's much better to use silica gel packets or air dry the phone instead."

I nodded and pretended that I had understood the kid's explanation. "Mainly, I'd like to know any phone numbers that were called frequently. Of course, pictures would help, too."

"I'll be in touch."

After he left, I felt slightly optimistic about gaining more information. I hoped I wouldn't be disappointed.

CHAPTER 13

I BROUGHT MY LUNCH TO WORK every day and usually ate it standing at the counter between customers. The lunch *hour* that I once enjoyed as a banker has shrunken to frantic bites when time allowed. The positive side to this arrangement is that I discovered pre-made salads that only required a packet of dressing and a fork, so my health has actually benefited from my lack of dining time. To compensate for my abbreviated mid-day meal, Harri and I tried to enjoy one dinner each week at a decent restaurant, the kind of place where you can order a beautifully plated entrée and a glass of wine, enjoy the atmosphere, and still leave without feeling like you've splurged too much.

This evening, Harri lifted her head from the wine list when our waiter arrived and ordered something good but not extravagant. It complemented our seared salmon with citrus glaze, which arrived as we traded stories from the day—some funny, some mildly exasperating, but all softened by the comfort of sharing with someone who *gets* it.

"I like this place." Harri sighed as she watched a tray of desserts parade by. I agreed, inhaling a faint garlic aroma wafting from the kitchen and eyeing the warm lighting, polished wood, crisp linens, and menu that were refined without requiring a second mortgage.

Harri excused herself as I finished my wine and felt my shoulders relax in that subtle shift from "on the clock" to "on my own." When she returned to the table, Harri's excitement had ratcheted far above my relaxation.

"You'll never guess who I ran into in the ladies' restroom."

I nodded. "Probably not."

"Amber, the dancer from Starbutts Men's Club." Harri beamed.

"Here? How in the world did you recognize her? Was she wearing clothes?"

Harri arched an eyebrow. "*She* was the one who recognized *me*, although I noticed she still wore those precariously high heels."

I raised my glass to her in a toast. "My dear, I have always said that you are a woman who is impossible to forget."

During a hair comb and a hand wash, Amber approached my wife and asked if Harri knew anything more about the death of her friend.

"Isn't this kind of a pricey place for her to be dining?"

I interrupted. "The tips at Starbutts must be pretty darn good these days. If they cancel your newspaper column, you might consider dancing on the side to boost our income."

Harri's nostrils flared, and she ignored my career suggestion. "I suspect Amber didn't come here alone."

Her suspicion proved to be well-founded. As we stood to leave, I spotted Amber settled in a quiet corner booth, her face illuminated by the flickering candle on the table. She was hard to miss—my wife failed to mention the bold, attention-grabbing outfit that clung to her form. When Amber saw Harri, she smiled and raised her hand for a quick wave. Her companion turned toward the wall as though admiring a piece of artwork and reached for his water glass, using it as a shield. He lifted it just high enough to obscure a large part of his face, but not the large gold signet ring that glinted on his little finger.

It was Alberto Raffo.

CHAPTER 14

"ARE WE IN A BIG hurry to get home tonight? You practically dragged me out to the parking lot."

Harri turned to face me as I reached for her car door.

"No, I was just in a hurry to leave the restaurant. Did you happen to notice Amber's dining companion?"

Harri clicked her seatbelt. "You didn't give me enough time to notice *anything,* Sir Speedy."

I slid behind the steering wheel and started the ignition. "She was sitting with Dr. Alberto Raffo."

Harri's mouth opened, then closed. "Do you think he noticed us as we were leaving?"

"I can't be certain, of course, but his body language indicated that he didn't want to be seen by *anyone.* He definitely tried to hide his face, which begs the question, Why?"

She turned to face me. "Well, for starters, I'm sure his wife would not be pleased to learn about his dinner date. My God, poor Joan. First Nikki Smith and now Amber?"

"We shouldn't jump to conclusions," I said. "There

may be a perfectly reasonable explanation."

Harri practically levitated out of her seat, and her voice bordered on a shout. "Really? Do you think she was trying to sell him some Girl Scout Cookies? Have you gone completely mad, Baxter?"

"No, dear, I'm just trying to be analytical. They do have something, or *someone,* in common, and that is Nikki Smith."

"*Was* Nikki Smith," Harri corrected.

"Amber might be blackmailing Alberto. Or she might be in trouble."

"And we know that Dr. Raffo does seem to be devoted to wayward girls," Harri said with a frown. "But Amber appeared to be smart and observant. Maybe she's been quietly gathering information about Starbutt's clientele."

"Forgive me, Sweetie, but that young woman does not seem bright enough to be a successful blackmailer."

"We're being analytical, remember? I'm considering all possibilities other than the obvious choice that Dr. Raffo is a pig and a serial philanderer."

"Okay, maybe she needed his medical opinion on a health issue?"

Harri shook her head. "That's what his office is for. Or did you happen to notice a stethoscope hanging around his neck?"

I grinned. "I did not."

A working silence settled between us, and I could almost hear the soft hum of my wife's mental calculations, the quiet tug of worry, and the subtle hope that one of us might find the missing piece. Passing traffic noise became a kind of backdrop to our shared concentration. Every so often, Harri inhaled like she was about to speak, then exhaled instead, still thinking.

"Maybe it's just two people orbiting the same absence," Harri offered as we pulled in the driveway. "Amber misses her friend, and maybe Alberto misses her too."

"That would be the kindest and simplest explanation," I said, though I thought it also might be the most unlikely.

CHAPTER 15

IN SPITE OF ITS QUIRKS, the job of harbormaster at a marina frequently reminded me how fortunate I was to have escaped my former life in corporate banking. Along with wearing a suit and tie, I didn't miss the unspoken competition among executives to see whose car arrived in the parking garage *first* every morning. That show of dedication was followed by an evening competition called "Whose car was the *last* to leave at the end of each day?"

But topping my list of annoyances was attendance at mandatory social events hosted by a senior officer. People with nothing in common—except their employer—were forced to socialize together during long, tedious evenings while remaining relatively sober. My current role brought some respite from those obligations. However, Peter Johnson's annual party was unavoidable. Rumor had it that the date coincided with his birthday; however, the formal invitations mailed to guests every year showed no indication of it. I would prefer to decline, but Harri insisted that skipping such an event could be perceived negatively, labeling me as "not a team player" or an "anti-social outlier."

"Well, I don't find either of those titles objectionable."

She squeezed my arm. "Think of this as an opportunity to build rapport that might lead to more effective communication between you and Peter."

"Has someone hired you to write an employee handbook for their human resources department?" I inquired. "We both know that Peter is incapable of effective communication unless it's in front of a judge and a jury."

Harri scoffed, but on the night of the party, I decided that the slinky black dress she wore was ample reward for donning the suit and tie previously buried in the back of my closet. I vowed to engage in pleasant conversation all evening with anyone who crossed my path.

The evening was warm and fragrant with salty air when we arrived at Peter's stunning waterfront mansion. The estate was a vision of elegance—its grand French doors thrown open to reveal a seamless flow between opulent interior spaces and expansive terraces that overlooked the shimmering bay. Inside, crystal chandeliers cast golden light across polished marble floors and velvet-upholstered furniture in deep jewel tones. Outside, lanterns swayed gently from pergolas, their glow mirrored in the still water below.

"I'll bet that Claire studies every single issue of

Architectural Digest religiously," Harri whispered.

We mingled with other guests in cocktail attire, and the clink of glasses rose above the soft strains of a live jazz quartet tucked beneath a flowering arbor. Waiters in crisp white jackets glided through the crowd with silver trays balanced expertly in hand. They offered flutes of chilled champagne, delicate canapés topped with caviar and edible flowers, and miniature desserts that looked like works of art from a museum.

"Perhaps I should have studied law instead of journalism," Harri mused.

I spotted Peter's children standing beside a lavish buffet table and decided it was time to eat something more substantial than hors d'oeuvres. Daniel immediately put his plate down, pulled out his phone, and showed me a beautiful drone video of a yacht underway in the marina's channel. The dramatic aerial view captured the beauty of the boat in its environment. "This one's for sale, and the yacht broker hired me to film it," he said with pride.

After watching the "bird's-eye view" of the yacht gliding through the water, I had to admit, the boy had some talent as a photographer. He was vastly different from my own son, who had majored in finance and was successfully climbing the corporate ladder.

Harri hugged Angela, who bore little resemblance to the girl I usually saw working at the marina. Tonight, she wore a pale pink cocktail dress that flattered her figure and caught the light with every movement. The fabric shimmered subtly, hinting at elegance without being ostentatious. Her makeup was tastefully done: a sweep of rose gold eyeshadow, a touch of blush on her cheekbones, and a pale pink lipstick that complemented her natural beauty. Her hair was styled in loose waves, cascading over her shoulders with effortless grace. She wore a pair of pearl and diamond earrings—probably her mother's—and a dainty bracelet that glinted as she gestured politely during conversation. Her smile was warm and genuine as she greeted her parents' guests, making eye contact and asking thoughtful questions. She appeared to be a miniature version of her mother—poised, articulate, and gracious.

Her mother clearly appreciated Angela's efforts. Claire, beaming proudly, excused herself from another conversation and slipped an arm around her daughter's waist

"It's wonderful to have our college girl home with us," she said with a smile.

"And I love having your daughter working at the marina," I replied as Angela blushed. For a moment, I wondered how Claire had behaved when she was her daughter's age, but the image didn't last long. I caught a reflection of the pair in a large, gilded mirror over the buffet and noticed that Angela was standing exactly the way her mother was—shoulders back, chin lifted. For a moment, they looked like two versions of the same woman, one polished by time, the other still learning the choreography.

When Harri excused herself to find a bathroom, I strolled to the backyard for a bit of fresh air and solitude. It was a night of effortless glamor, where every detail—from the flicker of candlelight to the sparkle of diamonds—felt like part of a carefully orchestrated symphony of indulgence designed to impress Peter's clients, friends, and a select few employees like me, who received one of the coveted invitations.

Despite the gilded surroundings, it was the sound of waves lapping against Peter's dock that beckoned me. I avoided the guests gathered near the infinity pool, its edge blending into the horizon. Instead, I stood alone and watched the water without noticing that, in the shadow of the boathouse, sat Alberto Raffo.

"Good evening, Baxter. Are you enjoying Peter's annual ode to extravagance?"

His tie was loosened like it had enough of the evening, too. He sat hunched on the edge of an Adirondack chair, nursing a half-empty glass like it was the only thing keeping him tethered. His eyes were distant, rimmed with a quiet ache, and every so often he stared into the drink as if searching for something lost. His movements were slow, deliberate, and there was a heaviness to him, as if each gesture cost more than it should.

"You don't need to save me dock space at the marina. I don't think I'll be buying another boat." His speech was soft, slurred not from excess but from exhaustion.

I nodded and waited through his long, thoughtful silence.

"She was a great girl and I . . . I only wanted to help."

When he spoke, it was in fragments—half-thoughts, unfinished sentences, memories he didn't seem sure that he wanted to share.

"Nikki was leaving, you know. Moving out of state or maybe out of the country, for all I know. I only let her stay aboard because she said it was temporary." He smiled, but it was hollow, a reflex more than a feeling. The flush in his cheeks might come from the alcohol, but the sadness in his posture was unmistakable. He was quietly unraveling, one sip at a time.

"I can't believe that she died on my boat. I suppose I realized the risk to my family too late."

I slid into the empty chair next to him.

"I understand. And I don't believe the police are convinced it was a suicide. Did you know Nikki very long?"

"Almost a year, I think. We met when I attended a stag party for one of my young associates at the place where she worked. I hadn't planned to . . ."

I sat quietly for a moment, absorbing the weight of the confession.

"It wasn't just a mistake. It was selfish. I knew what I was doing, and I did it anyway." His voice cracked. "Her friend blames me and, in some ways, she's right."

I studied his face for a moment and said, "We all make mistakes. But in my experience, rumors ruin far more reputations than reality."

Alberto leaned back in his chair and closed his eyes. "My life is a mess. Joan can barely stand to look at me."

I stood and faced the water until a shift in the air—subtle, but the unmistakable whisper of Prada perfume drifted past my nose. That perfume. Her perfume, the one that lingered on my collar long after she left the room. I turned and found Harri waiting just behind me, with that quiet smile that always said more than words ever could.

"You always find me."

"I never stop looking," she replied. "But I didn't want to interrupt your conversation with Alberto. I spent some time with Joan Raffo, but our conversation was short and more formal. It definitely lacked her usual warmth. I got the impression that she was struggling to maintain her dignity in a fairly public setting."

She reached for my hand. "Have you had enough fun for one evening, my darling?"

We timed our exit between the clink of champagne flutes and a burst of laughter from the far end of Peter's massive living room. We moved with quiet precision, like dancers slipping offstage before the final bow. Harri had mastered the art of polite nods and half-smiles that suggested presence without permanence. A waiter passed, his eyes flicking toward us, but said nothing—perhaps recognizing the look of guests who'd had enough of gilded conversation and curated charm.

Outside, the night air had turned crisp by the time we walked to our car, which I'd parked outside the estate walls in anticipation of an easy escape. Harri's heels clicked softly on the paved brick driveway as she glanced my way. In her grin, I detected equal parts relief and rebellion.

CHAPTER 16

BRIEFLY ESCAPING FROM HIS DUTIES in the boatyard, Gordon stopped in my office for coffee shortly before Linda arrived with a magazine article touting Florida's top marinas.

"Gentlemen, you'll be pleased to know that our own Moss Creek Marina made the cut."

I grinned, appreciating the banter that routinely filled the dockmaster's office. It had become a place for swapping sea tales, joking about boat mishaps, and bonding over many similar challenges. This camaraderie was less about our formal roles at the marina and more about a shared way of life—weathered by salt, shaped by tides, and anchored in mutual care.

Since Harri had an early meeting with her editor and left our house before I did, I was surprised to see her appear at my impromptu office party.

"Good morning, everyone. I'm afraid there's been a leak in the marina's code of silence. Has anyone else seen this social media post?"

Harri held up her phone, the screen displaying a grainy screenshot of a Reddit post from an anonymous account. The title read: *Who Killed Nikki Smith?*

The post continued with cryptic language: *She's gone, and no one's talking. If you know anything, please DM me. This doesn't feel right.*

"That post went up three hours ago," Harri said, squinting at the screen. "It's already got over 200 comments. Evidently, Nikki had quite a following at Starbutts."

I sensed the tension as Gordon exchanged an uneasy glance with Linda, who whispered, "Do you think you should tell Peter?"

But no one moved. The screen glowed in Harri's hand, casting a pale light over the group.

I cleared my throat. "I guess that would be up to me. Can you text me that screenshot?"

I waited until after lunch to break the news.

Approaching a mercurial boss like Peter usually involved a quiet, gnawing dread in my gut—an emotional tightrope walk where every step felt uncertain. One day, he was jovial and generous; the next, he was curt and cutting. Over the years, I learned to read subtle cues to deal with his mood roulette: the sharpness in his greeting or his lack of eye contact. It was like walking on eggshells, so I rehearsed my words, second-guessed my tone, and braced for impact.

My heart raced as I knocked on his door, and I imagined every possible reaction, most of them bad. I wasn't just delivering unfortunate news—I was navigating a minefield of ego, volatility, and fear.

"Hey Peter, have you got a minute?"

He read the post over and over, dissecting every word, convinced it was part of a conspiracy. "I want the author identified, tracked, and dealt with—whether it's a customer, an employee, or a random nut who read about it in the newspaper."

Peter shouted loud enough to rattle the blinds, demanding to know "who let this happen" as if betrayal lurked in every corner. It wasn't long before he threatened legal action, PR blitzes, firings—he threw out plans like grenades, most of them half-baked and impossible. It wasn't just anger—it was a spectacle. His reaction wasn't about the post itself, but the threat to his image, his control, and his fragile sense of invincibility.

"Peter, I believe we need to uncover the truth about Nikki's death to bring a killer to justice, protect our customers, and preserve the marina's safety and reputation. Failure risks further violence, legal exposure for this marina, and potential harm to the community."

He glared and tossed the phone at me like it was radioactive. After enough negative encounters like this, I might start avoiding him altogether.

When I arrived back at my own office, a young man was waiting for me. For one fleeting moment, I wondered who ordered DoorDash. Then I noticed the plastic bag holding a purple glitter phone case and realized I was speaking with the digital forensics expert recommended by Tom McDonald.

I shook his hand. "Good to see you again."

He handed me a printed document. "I used a clean room environment and specialized imaging tools to extract fragments of the device's internal storage. In spite of its scorched exterior, the phone yielded critical data thanks to some of my advanced extraction techniques. From the recovered data, I compiled a list of the most frequently dialed numbers. These were cross-referenced with time-stamps and call durations to establish communication patterns."

I marveled at his efficiency, even if I didn't completely understand it.

He concluded with a nod: "Even in extreme conditions, digital traces persist. I hope it helps provide leads in the broader investigation."

My next call was to Detective Joe Squires to tell him I'd discovered the cell phone.

As I neared the end of my shift, I compared the list of phone numbers that I'd been given with the contact information in our marina records. Almost immediately,

I identified Albert Raffo's number, but another one appeared even more frequently. I decided to call it and see who might answer. Just after I punched in the number, I saw Angela walking along the dock, headed to work. She reached into her jeans pocket and pulled out her phone.

"Hello?" echoed in my ear.

The recognition washed through me like a soft wave.

"Ahh, Angela. It's Cap'n Mac. Just checking to be sure you're working tonight."

She opened the office door with a grin. "Have I ever let you down?"

CHAPTER 17

IN MY HASTE TO SPEAK with my wife, I let our front door slam behind me. Harri woke up with a start after falling asleep at her desk, the space bar clearly imprinted on her forehead.

"I'm desperately in need of your wise counsel," I said, taking a long swig of the Blue Moon I'd just pulled from our refrigerator.

"Then I'll forgive you for starting tonight's cocktail hour without me." She reached for a wine glass and a bottle opener.

I described calling the phone number retrieved from Nikki's cell phone and discovering that it belonged to Angela.

"Well, the girls are about the same age. Why wouldn't they chat at night during Angela's shift? Most evenings the marina is pretty quiet, so they'd have plenty of time to talk and build a friendship."

I swallowed. "I don't mean just as friends. Do

you . . . Do you think Angela might have been . . . ahhh, romantically involved with Nikki?"

Harri paused, Sauvignon Blanc bottle in hand, considering. She didn't look shocked; she just looked thoughtful.

"If she were, she would have good reason to stay silent. I doubt that her parents would understand or be supportive of the relationship."

She stepped closer, resting her hand on my arm.

"It might also explain why Angela never spends too much time with her family in Florida, why she prefers to travel and surf throughout the world. I'm not sure that Peter and Claire understand that you can't choose who your child loves. You can only choose to support them."

I pulled Harri into my arms. Her empathy wasn't just words; it was a reflection of her character, a quiet strength that made others feel seen and valued. In that moment, I felt proud to walk through life beside the woman whose kindness could soften the hardest edges of the world, and I cherished the grace with which she extended love not only to our own children, but to everyone who needed it.

"You are a compassionate woman, Harriet McCracken," I said as I kissed the top of her head. "That's why I fell in love with you in the first place."

"Liar," she whispered, tilting her chin upward for a real kiss. "My compassion had nothing to do with it."

The next morning, I was happy to see Detective Joe Squires at my office and even happier to hand over the plastic bag containing the glittery cell phone.

"We'll check on the girl's digital dust. That's a term for all the markers we leave in our lives all over the place, whenever we drive, pay for something or make a call. Every time we text, email, visit a website, post on social media, or appear in someone else's post, we leave a trail. In a wired world, our digital dust stays with every 'like' or page visit. If we collect that dust and sweep it into a pile, it offers a pretty detailed picture of someone's life."

I nodded and asked if there were any new leads in the investigation. He admitted arson investigators determined the fire started *on* deck, not *below* deck in the cabin. He also mentioned a dud round of ammunition was discovered in the charred cabin—accidentally ignited by the flames— along with ballistic residue, which proved the doctor's early admission that he kept firearms on board.

"Well, Detective, we've all heard about pirates of the Caribbean."

Joe Squires shot me a sideways glance.

"I haven't seen any of them lately, Cap'n Mac." He poured himself a cup of coffee in an *It's Better in the Bahamas* mug. "We need a warrant to get somebody's phone location history, but I'd be curious to know where the victim's phone has traveled. Of course, we'll be reviewing recent communications to see who she contacted before the incident."

I didn't mention that I already knew.

Steam curled upward, but the detective didn't drink—just stared into the coffee as though it might offer answers he hadn't already chased for too many years. "That Starbutts Men's Club is bad news. A victim was discovered in a car parked behind the club two days ago. Probably one of the dancers."

I leaned an elbow on the counter as if I was just making conversation. "Really? How did the woman die?"

The detective exhaled slowly, the kind of sigh that carried more weight than sound. "The pathologist hasn't issued a formal cause of death yet. But what I read in the preliminary report indicates it was probably a drug over-dose. The skin and lips looked bluish, and there were no signs of a struggle."

"Does the victim have a name?"

Joe Squires paused and ran his thumb around the rim of the mug. "It was some kind of mineral like amethyst—no amber. The woman's name was Amber."

CHAPTER 18

I STARED AT THE DETECTIVE. "I'VE actually met that girl. In fact, my wife and I saw her only a week ago, having dinner with Alberto Raffo."

Squires looked up from his coffee, his attention focused, and I felt an odd sense of pressure to be extra careful or precise in whatever I said next. "My wife ran into her in the ladies' room, and Amber asked if we knew anything more about the death of her friend, Nikki."

"How does your wife know the victim?"

"Well, detective, I wouldn't say that we *know* her, but we met the girl when my wife—her name is Harriet—and I visited Starbutts Men's Club."

Squire's eyebrows lifted, creating a brief ripple across his forehead. It was the kind of movement that happened before he could stop it, a reflexive "Wait, what?"

I stammered on. "We went one afternoon to learn more about the dancer who died in the boat fire here, at the marina. We only spoke to the girl, Amber, briefly when she came to our table.”

Squire's lips parted slightly, not enough to speak yet, just enough to show he wasn't anticipating what he just heard.

"All right, in your *brief* meeting, how did the victim appear to you?"

I described our conversation, including Amber's denial that her former roommate used drugs as well as her suspicion that her friend no longer relied on dancing at Starbutts to support herself.

"In fact, the only thing she indulged in while we were with her was a vape pen."

There was a pause, a beat of silence, where Squires was clearly processing this new information.

"I appreciate your frankness," he said, eyes steady. "For now, don't make any vacation plans with your wife. We may need to follow up with you, and it's important you're available."

He didn't raise his voice or sound threatening—he didn't need to. His authority was built into the phrasing, the cadence, the expectation that this wasn't a suggestion. Then he added, more matteroffact than menacing, "If we have more questions, we'll be in touch. Make sure we can reach you."

It was time to reassess everything I thought I understood about the case, the relationships, and the stakes.

I wondered whether the two deaths were connected, and if so, how. What were the hidden connections between those young women—shared enemies, shared secrets, or a coverup?

During my rounds, I spotted Tom McDonald wielding a hose while Jimmy Buffett songs floated from below deck. "Got a minute?"

I told him about my visit from the detective and the victim discovered in the strip club parking lot.

Tom spoke in that calm-but-firm tone that law enforcement officers use when they want to sound polite without leaving any room for misunderstanding.

"My friend, the Florida Department of Health's statistics on unintentional or undetermined drug overdose deaths would curl your hair. The opioid crisis, synthetic drugs, and God only knows what new, emerging substances are sold on the street destroy a lot of lives in our state. One of the biggest contributors to the rise in overdose deaths is fentanyl, a synthetic opioid that's 50 to 100 times more potent than *morphine*. Many victims don't even realize they are taking it because it's laced with something else, like cannabis. In my years on the force, the situation didn't end well."

By the end of the day, I felt as though I had a tight band wrapped around my head. I recognized the signs of a tension headache—the dull, aching pressure rather than sharp or throbbing pain. I bought a small packet of pain relievers that we stocked for marina guests, petted the cat, and hurried to my car.

There had been no time to let Harri know about Amber's death, but I believed some news was best delivered in person.

I found her in the kitchen, with her sleeves pushed up and hair pinned back. The cutting board was crowded—romaine, cherry tomatoes, cucumbers, red onion, peppers, and herbs. Enough for a salad big enough to feed the neighborhood. After a kiss and a quick sip from the bottle of Peroni I pulled from the refrigerator, I outlined the news I'd heard only hours earlier.

Harri's breath caught. "What . . . what happened?"

"They don't know yet, but she was found behind Starbutts Gentleman's Club in her car two days ago."

The kitchen felt suddenly too quiet, the hum of the refrigerator unbearably loud. Harri pressed her palms against the counter, grounding herself. "She was just a kid . . . about the same age as our own."

I stepped around the island and pulled her into my arms. She stood rigid, as if her body hadn't caught up to the news. "Do you think it's just a coincidence? Two girls who worked together and were friends are both dead."

I shook my head. "I don't know. The detective said it looked like a drug overdose."

"I suppose it's possible. We didn't exactly *know* the girl, or her habits, did we?"

We stood there in the fading light, dinner forgotten, the world suddenly feeling more fragile than it had an hour ago.

CHAPTER 19

I WAS READY FOR A BEER and some decent barbecue. One more loop around the docks, and my shift was over. Harri would be waiting for me in my office. The sun was beginning to set, so I left my hat on a chair to better enjoy the evening breeze. I love the marina at dusk. It's like being in the ocean on my old surfboard. It's just so quiet to be out there, part of the ocean and yet apart from it. The first two docks looked impeccable—no trip hazards, water hoses coiled, fenders in place, no boats listing or stuck under the dock. I heard my stomach begin to growl.

On the third, a covered dock, I spotted a problem. Well, not a problem, but a pet peeve of mine, and I stooped to re-cleat a tangled line. It's fairly simple, but some people tie their ropes in a kind of macrame mess, which makes it extremely difficult to remove from the cleat if you need to, in a hurry. As I tightened the last loop, I was careful to keep the moldy rope away from my pants and shirt sleeves (which might necessitate a change of clothing before Harri and I could head out for that barbecue). I was almost finished when I heard the rhythmic creaking of wooden planks and felt a swish of air before a sharp, searing pain exploded at the back of my head. The world around me faded into a dark abyss.

"Captain Mac? Captain Mac? Oh my, I am so sorry. Can you hear me?" Slowly, I watched Linda's face come into focus. She clutched a plastic grocery bag filled with canned goods that continued to drop with loud thuds onto the dock beside me. "I didn't know it was *you*. You're not wearing your big hat. I thought someone was trying to steal my boat. Oh my, please get up. Are you okay? Should I call 911?"

I struggled to sit up and felt the lump forming on my head. At least there was no blood on my hand, no need for a trip to the emergency room, which might seriously delay my dinner.

Angela stood at the counter, flicking the blade of a Swiss Army knife dangerously close to her wrist.

"Captain Mac is finishing his last rounds." Her voice shook a little, and she refused to meet Harri's eyes.

"Then I'll just wait for him here with you," Harri

said, as she glanced at the ship's-wheel clock on the wall, feeling mildly concerned that her husband was running late.

Angela sat on the wooden counter stool, slowly circling to the left, then to the right. "My mother always tried to drown my words with wine. I bet you're a great mom."

She described her life, present and past: the migration of her friends to jobs across the country, taking breaks from college and living under her parents' roof, unable to date whom she wanted because she knew that Claire and Peter would disapprove.

"At college, I felt free. But when I come home, I become someone else. I edit my stories and change the pronouns. It's like living in two worlds that absolutely cannot touch. My parents don't yell or scream at me. They just go quiet, and that silence is louder than any argument we could have. It tells me I'm wrong, that I've disappointed them. And that hurts more than I ever thought it could."

Her life sounded to Harri like a steady erosion of opportunity and hope.

After a pause, Angela continued. "I was on the boat the night Nikki died, and I tried to talk to her, but she was drinking. I'd seen the doctor leave, and I couldn't believe that she might be *with* him, you know? Nikki loved *me*, and we were going away together. We planned a whole new life in another country, away from here, away from my family. We finally had a chance to be happy."

She tugged on her faded hoodie and wrapped it tightly around her, as though the knit fabric might keep her from falling apart. "I just wanted Nikki to look me in the eye. I needed her to *explain.* Part of me was desperate to be convinced that, despite how it looked, she was somehow innocent. The idea that she might still be involved with that creepy old guy . . . You know that he's a friend of my father, right? It was just unthinkable."

She struggled to get her emotions under control. After several deep breaths, Angela continued. "I guess in some ways, the doctor was better than that girl, *Amber.* At least he gave Nikki a free place to stay, and I would never have met her if she hadn't come to the marina. Even then, after we got together, Amber kept pestering Nikki to go back to working nights at Starbutts. After she died, I finally met up with Amber to pick up a few things Nikki had left at the club. It was just some clothes and makeup, and a little stuffed dolphin I'd given to her. But it was all I had left because everything else burned in the boat fire."

She closed her eyes as if trying to erase the image in her mind. "Amber sounded okay on the phone, but when I got there, she started throwing things and screaming that I was the reason Nikki was dead. She was acting crazy. I ducked once and noticed some pill bottles beside the makeup mirror, so I dropped a couple in her drink so that I could get back to my car in one piece. She practically attacked me in the parking lot."

Harri nodded and slid gently onto the stool opposite Angela, careful not to interrupt the girl's flow of words. When she raised her eyes, tears splashed on Angela's jeans, darkening the denim. Harri thought the girl resembled an animal trapped in a holding pen, waiting to be slaughtered.

"The night of the fire, Nikki laughed at me, *laughed*, and I got mad. I walked the docks for a while, just tried to breathe, and when I came back, the boat was quiet. I thought she was asleep, and I wanted to teach her a lesson, so just before my shift ended, I untied the lines. I was angry, so I pushed the boat off the dock and watched the current carry it out. Nikki doesn't—didn't—know anything about running a boat. I wanted her to wake up alone and feel afraid."

Harri sucked in her breath and held it. Her right hand pressed against her chest, trying to muffle the sound of her racing heart.

"But that's so fucked up, because I'm the only one who's alone. *Again.*"

Angela wiped her right eye with the knuckle of her forefinger, then dried it in her lap as the tears came faster. She moved her hands up to her face, and her shoulders hunched as she began to sob. Harri walked around the counter and put her arms around the girl, but not before she slid the Swiss Army knife out of reach.

I burst through the office door to see that Angela wasn't just holding onto my wife; she was *clinging,* the way a drowning person might cling to a buoy.

"There you are, darling. So nice of you to join us at last. You must be very hungry." Her smile seemed somehow radiant and sad at once.

"I, uh, yeah." I grabbed a can of Coke from the glass case and pressed it to my head. Harri raised an eyebrow.

"Sorry, I'm late. I had a little accident on the dock."

Harri's look indicated that my explanation was insufficient, but she merely nodded and gave me an abbreviated version of Angela's confession.

"Will you be alright here tonight for your shift?" she asked softly, as she began to extricate herself from the girl.

When Angela raised her face toward Harri, her gaze was almost imploring. "I'm fine. I'll be fine."

I thought she looked utterly miserable.

"Of course you will be. But please call Baxter and me tonight if you need anything, okay?"

Harri was a natural mother, whether she gave birth to the child in question or not. I admired the nurturing side of my wife, although she rarely displayed it. Removing the cold can from my head, I leaned on the counter and looked directly at Angela.

"You must understand that none of this was your

fault. Untying a boat did not kill Nikki Smith. Angela, you are *not* responsible for her death."

Her lower lip quivered as she attempted to smile.

"I ... I guess I do understand. But that doesn't make it any easier."

CHAPTER 20

I WAS NOT SURPRISED WHEN ANGELA called in sick the next day. Fortunately, she asked her brother to cover her shift, and Daniel arrived with his drone in hand, which gave me some idea of the amount of work he might accomplish in the next eight hours. Still, his excitement was palpable.

"Cap'n Mac, you've got to see these videos. The footage I shot of the marina at night makes this place look better than Walt Disney World."

Indeed, the underwater lights featured on several of the yachts cast an otherworldly glow in the water. Even the dock lighting appeared to sparkle when viewed from above.

"Do you think my dad might want to use any of these for advertising on social media?" Daniel asked.

"You should ask him. For what it's worth, I would use these videos if I owned the marina."

A thought occurred to me, but I kept it to myself. It was far-fetched and highly unlikely to amount to much, but it was worth a shot. I hesitated, then cleared my throat and attempted nonchalance. "I was wondering . . . Do you have any more night footage of this place? Angela told me you've been out here filming on several evenings."

The young man's eyes lit up as he scrolled through the footage on his tablet, eager to share the sweeping aerial shots he had captured with his drone. He explained the angles he had chosen with a mix of pride and nervous energy. He described the way the evening light fell across the water, and the patterns he had noticed from above that most people never get to see. I leaned in attentively, nodding with genuine interest, and kept my expression warm and encouraging. That quiet appreciation made Daniel's delight grow even stronger—he felt not only validated in his artistic efforts but also connected, as if his vision had found a receptive audience who truly understood the beauty he was trying to reveal.

Inside, I wrestled with the possibility that the images might reveal what happened on the night *Feelin' Nauti* burned, but outwardly I remained composed, careful not to betray the urgency that stirred beneath the surface. I glanced at the dates and timestamps on each video until he arrived at the fateful night in question. The night he joined his sister during her shift to do some filming, and likely continued after she went home. At times, the vast expanse of water appeared almost black, reflecting faint glimmers of moonlight or distant stars. From some angles, the horizon outside the marina was barely visible, blending into the night sky. According to the timestamp, it was 6 a.m. when I spotted the Raffos' sailboat drifting in the channel, until a luminous V-shape cutting through the water—foamy and silver under the moonlight—approached. It was clearly the wake of another vessel.

I asked if we could get a closer look, and Daniel zoomed in to reveal someone standing in a craft whose hull I'd recognize anywhere: a Gheenoe with its soundless electric trolling motor.

"I shot this video just before sunrise," he said with a grin. "Isn't the light incredible?"

"Absolutely incredible," I answered. "Could you send me a copy of this?"

Daniel looked delighted. "Sure."

I wondered what Detective Joe Squires would think when he viewed the footage. I'd know soon enough.

He answered my call on the second ring and appeared at my marina the following day during an afternoon lull. My laptop sat open, and the detective leaned in, his notebook in hand. His expression sharpened when I clicked the play button. The drone footage began with a smooth aerial sweep over the marina: rows of boats bobbing gently, their masts like a forest of thin, wavering lines. Then the camera shifted, dipping toward the channel at the far end of the pier.

"Watch this part," I said, tapping the screen with a tense finger.

The policeman's jaw tightened. He paused the video, rewound a few seconds, and watched it again, this time at a slower pace.

"You said this was recorded that night," he said, not looking away from the screen.

I nodded. "Check the date and time stamp in the corner. One of my dockmasters was filming that night during his shift, but I didn't see the video until yesterday, just before I called you."

Outside, a gull screeched, and a sudden gust of wind rattled the office window. Inside, the room felt suddenly smaller, and the weight of what we had just seen settled between us like a thick fog. Even Marina sat up in her bed and stared at me.

"I'll need this video, of course."

"I understand, Detective. It's yours."

Moments after the detective left my office, the tension I'd been holding collapsed like a weight. A dull ache pulsed at the base of my neck, radiating upward in slow, punishing waves. I rolled my shoulders once, twice, but the muscles refused to loosen. Now that the telling was over, the exhaustion settled in—that heavy, bone-deep kind that made my limbs feel as though they were weighted. Less than an hour before my shift ended, a text from Harri appeared on my phone. *Love the new aerial footage on your Facebook page. Moss Creek Marina is getting a lot of likes.* Puzzled, I clicked on the app and was shocked to see that Daniel had uploaded his night video. Of course, he hadn't understood its contents, but the footage needed to be removed immediately.

More importantly, Peter needed to be told *why.* I headed for his office.

CHAPTER 21

With Peter's unpredictable moods, I was never sure if I would be met with praise or reprimand. In this situation, I figured my odds were 50/50 either way. But the truth mattered, even if delivering it felt like stepping into a lion's den.

I replayed the facts in my mind, rehearsed the phrasing, and wondered if there was a gentler way to say something that simply wasn't gentle. The number of things I'd failed to grasp was as limitless as the stars in the night sky. It seemed as though Alberto had collected regrets while Joan gathered resentment.

Nevertheless, I was surprised to see both of them sitting in Peter's office when I arrived to deliver the news. The uncomfortable silence that followed indicated they were equally surprised to see me.

I cleared my throat. "I'm not sure who's handling the marina's social media accounts these days, but there's a video posted that your son, Daniel, shot with his drone, and it needs to be taken down."

Peter's eyes were expressionless, but his jaw was clenched. I continued, "The video was taken on the night that Dr. and Mrs. Raffo's boat burned."

Alberto turned to stare at me, waiting for me to go on. Perhaps afraid of where I was headed.

"The police have a copy of the footage in their possession and will be contacting you soon. That is, if they haven't already, Mrs. Raffo."

All eyes turned to Joan, and I watched her sit a little straighter. She gave me a long, steady look. "We always think that answers will fix everything, Baxter. But they don't. Someone once said that information is power. But it's also a burden, because once you know something . . . you can't overlook it."

She paused. "I knew about Alberto's affairs," she said, staring at her husband. "All of them."

I couldn't see his face, but a flush crept up Alberto's neck, and his posture stiffened.

Joan perched on the edge of Peter's office couch as though the cushions might swallow her if she leaned back. Her fingers were laced tightly in her lap, and her voice sounded steady at first—almost too steady, the way someone sounds when they've rehearsed a speech alone for years. But as she spoke, the exhaustion behind her eyes became unmistakable. I couldn't help but feel the slow erosion that happened when trust was chipped away one quiet betrayal at a time.

I waited for her to cry, but Joan looked like a woman who had run out of tears long before today.

"I didn't realize anyone was on board," she said, turning to Peter, her eyes pleading. "I saw the boat drifting, and I was *glad* because I knew it would upset Alberto if it ran aground and was damaged. That stupid boat, the one I never wanted, gave him freedom. When I think of all of his lies . . . I paddled alongside it, and that's when I saw the cell phone, so I grabbed it to prove that another woman had been there."

She stood up and began to pace. "You have no idea what my life has been like. I was so angry and upset and then . . . Then I saw the gas can at the stern that Alberto kept for emergencies, and this seemed like an emergency. I remember tilting it a little, letting the liquid spill across the deck. Every splash felt like a strike against Alberto, a punishment for his years of betrayal. I decided that if he wouldn't get rid of his *women*, I'd get rid of his *boat*. It seemed like the perfect solution for our problems. I must have spilled a little in the water because I remember seeing a few shimmering trails that caught the moonlight like silver streaks."

A faint smile curved upward at the memory, even as tears welled in the corners of her eyes. She faced Peter, shaking slightly. "I swear, I had no idea that girl was still on board. Peter, you *know* me. Please, I need your help."

Peter leaned back in his chair, distancing himself physically even as the emotional gravity seemed to pull him forward. Looking at my boss, I saw a man walking a tight-rope—balancing duty, emotion, and the weight of a past relationship—while trying to maintain the cool, analytical exterior expected of a defense attorney.

I wanted nothing more than to bolt out of the door, out of the office, and out of the terrible truth I had just heard. "I, ah, I'll leave you to it and head back to my office."

Walking the docks, I watched as my marina kept moving—ropes tightening, engines rumbling, crews polishing their teak decking—yet it felt as though the world should have stopped, just for a moment, to acknowledge what had happened.

But the world didn't stop. It never did.

A gull shrieked overhead, and I flinched just as the VHF radio on my belt crackled. "Cap'n Mac, we've got a customer at the fuel dock who needs your assistance."

I closed my eyes. Just for a heartbeat. Just long enough to imagine walking away—past the yachts, past the seawall, down the road toward home, where I could finally process the day's events. But when I opened them, the boats were still there, the marina still humming, and my duties still waiting.

At home, hot shower spray hissed against the tile walls where I stood, and I savored the solitude. Unresolved conflict spreads like cancer in human relationships, and sometimes, I decided, there was no cure. The fabric of the relationship between Joan and Alberto had been repeatedly stretched, torn, and restitched over the years. A patchwork quilt of love and lies born out of duty and expectation, I supposed. We all have our version of the truth, and I suspect that it's rarely complete.

I pulled on a clean shirt and a fresh pair of shorts, sipped my beer, and considered ordering pizza for dinner. Outside, the sky had turned pinkish purple, and the scent of Confederate jasmine filled the backyard by the time Harri joined me on the sofa.

"I can't imagine her pain, but I also can't imagine his continuous cheating," she said after listening to an abbreviated version of my day. "Even if Alberto is genuinely sorry, that doesn't mean everything can be forgiven. For some mistakes, particularly *repeated* ones, there is no statute of limitations. I'm worried about Joan—do you think she will go to prison?"

"She asked Peter to represent her today, and I suspect the charge would be manslaughter," I said. "Even though the outcome is still tragic—a young woman's life was lost—a jury might recognize that she didn't act with the deliberate, premeditated mindset required for a murder charge."

"It sounds like you've been listening to your sheriff friend Tom McDonald, I see."

"Indeed, he has been a wealth of information for this lowly harbormaster," I acknowledged. "It's like going back to college without textbooks or exams."

Harri laughed at the image of me as a college student.

"Have you ever been tempted to have an affair?"

"Never." I draped my arm around her shoulders and squeezed them. "Who could compare?"

"My darling husband, you have an amazing grasp of the obvious. But if you did stray, I certainly wouldn't try to kill my competition."

She cocked her head. *"You,* possibly. But definitely not the other woman."

"Why don't I find that reassuring?"

She wagged her finger at me. "It wasn't intended to be."

We sat in silence for a while, and I counted the blessings that I usually took for granted. The simple truth about life is that you forget most of it. The painful things you believed that you would never get over? In time, you won't remember exactly when they occurred. Many of my own memories—both good and bad—have been replaced by new experiences and new delights.

As the sun ducked below the palm trees on the horizon, Harri's voice blossomed into a smile, and she lifted a glass to her lips. "Here's to us. And let's give our children a call."

Acknowledgements

You are truly a good friend and an avid reader if you're here with me in the acknowledgments. And, as an avid reader, you know that a complete book doesn't burst from the brain of an author in perfect form and ready to print.

Agatha Christie only needed "a steady table and a typewriter." I required a supply of legal pads, pens, pocket notebooks, a computer, and occasional assistance overcoming writer's block.

That's why I am so grateful for my talented, crazy, supportive, and mostly sober friends who encouraged me to complete the manuscript that I'd talked about for far too long. That includes my fellow board members at the Florida Authors and Publishers Association, who inspire me daily with their commitment to helping both novice and seasoned authors with industry changes and challenges. In particular, I'd like to thank Anne Jacob of Popin Edits for her unfailing enthusiasm and critical eye. You made the book better in every way.

Nancy Koucky of NRK Designs created an amazing cover—using Bob Garrison's equally amazing photo! She and her husband, Chuck, are Pine Island residents who completely understand life on the waterfront.

And finally, my husband and co-author, who generously shared his marina experiences with me at the end of each day in great detail. You are the true harbormaster, and I am very lucky to be part of your crew.

About the Authors

RENEE GARRISON is a former reporter for The Tampa Tribune and the past president of the Florida Authors and Publishers Association. She has written two award-winning Young Adult books and traces her love for mysteries back to her early devotion to Nancy Drew books. She grew up spending summers on Cape Cod, where her love affair with coastal towns began, and moved to Florida before Walt Disney ever arrived.

ROBERT GARRISON is a fifth-generation Floridian whose love of the water began early—he earned his first boat at twelve by trading lawn-mowing work for the hull that set his course. After a successful career in finance, he spent nearly a decade as the harbormaster of a marina on Florida's East Coast, a role that deepened his connection to the tides and the people who live by them. He's never happier than when he's on the water or close enough to smell the salt in the air.